This Is the Way My Garden Grows

ALSO BY
BARBARA DODGE BORLAND

The Greater Hunger

W. W. NORTON & COMPANY
NEW YORK · LONDON

THIS IS THE WAY MY GARDEN GROWS

(and Comes into the Kitchen)

BARBARA DODGE BORLAND

Drawings by Lilly Langotsky

Published simultaneously in Canada by Penguin Books Canada Ltd.,
2801 John Street,
Markham, Ontario L3R 1B4
Printed in the United States of America.
The text of this book is composed in Goudy Old Style, with
display type set in Berling Roman. Composition and
manufacturing by The Maple-Vail Book Manufacturing Group.
Book design by Lilly Langotsky

First Edition

Library of Congress Cataloging-in-Publication Data
Borland, Barbara Dodge.
This is the way my garden grows—and comes into the kitchen.
Includes index.
1. Gardening.   2. Cookery (Vegetables),   I. Title.
SB453.B683   1986   635   85–29847

ISBN 0-393-02298-6

W. W. Norton & Company, Inc.
500 Fifth Avenue, New York, N.Y. 10110
W. W. Norton & Company Ltd.
37 Great Russell Street, London WC1B 3NU

1 2 3 4 5 6 7 8 9 0

FOR HAL

Contents

Sauces

Desserts

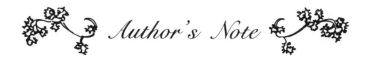

Author's Note

I love to garden. Ever since I had that first ridiculous 9′ by 12′ plot and planted seeds and found they grew, I have wanted—and actually needed—a garden wherever I lived. With the next five gardens I experimented and added in the mistakes and successes of the earlier gardens. The only trouble was that it took so much time to grow those vegetables and spend time on flowers, too. I had other things I wanted to do and I couldn't do everything at once. So I had to find short cuts and timesavers. I found out that I could shorten the garden labor. For instance, I learned that if I figured on three heavy planting days I only had to spend three half hours a week taking care of that garden.

My methods are completely different, contrary to most gardening directions, and completely original as far as I know. They work for me and for others who have tried them.

I use weeds for beneath-soil water even in a drought. My hoe-up system is to hoe up dirt against my vegetable plants to a specified height, to have weeds where I want them, and not where *they* want to be.

I found that if I planted in part rows, a third of a row, or even the length of a yardstick, and pulled out that crop just as soon as its heavy yield was over, I'd accomplish two things. First, I had a natural rotation of crops so the soil didn't need extra fertilizer. Second, by pulling out a finished crop like bush beans and planting a different vegetable in that same part row, I eliminated most of the bugs that attack plants.

I think my gardening *method* would work anywhere. Besides the six gardens that I have handled, I have included six extra gardens for other would-be gardeners, such as the Weekend Garden and the Summer-Away Garden. They worked! Gardening is such a mixture of mistakes and successes, and I often think the mistakes are the most important.

I also love to cook. And after all, when I put in that much time planning and planting and gathering luscious vegetables, I don't want them ruined by dreary cooking. Nor would you. Vegetable gardening goes hand-in-hand with vegetable cookery, I think. For each vegetable I have given cooking directions, and also some of the recipes I have concocted.

Barbara Dodge Borland
Salisbury, Connecticut

Part 1

A GARDENER LEARNS

seem to run into people all the time who say, one: "How I'd love to have a garden, but I just don't have the time." The second alibi is, "How I would like to grow vegetables, but I just don't know where to start."

I don't have the time either, but I make the time with a minimum of work and tending, thinking of those wonderful vegetables, envisioning the red ripe tomatoes, the succulent sweet corn, the tiny bush beans—and crunchy red radishes, cucumbers, and baby carrots. So I manage short cuts and ways to simplify the chores of weeding and tending. I think I can safely say that after planting, three half-hours a week is all that is necessary to keep that garden thriving.

I'm a dirt farmer. I like the feeling of soil crumbling between my fingers to tell me when it's time to plant. I like the feeling of working in a garden with sky above, sun all around me, and knowing that at my whim I can plant whatever I choose.

It's such fun to go out to your garden and select what you want for lunch or dinner instead of depending on the supermarket and paying atrocious prices for inferior quality.

Of course my fingernails are down to the quick, and if it's raining I get all muddy and my sneakers can sink and come halfway off. But the bounty is there. For free.

Flower gardening is a different thing. Flowers are beautiful in the house or outdoors but you can't eat flowers.

A gardener learns more in the mistakes than in the successes. Or so I found. And a gardener learns to be a philosopher, depending on weather—drought, windstorms, late frost or early frost—and who can control the weather?

MY FIRST GARDEN

My first garden was a catastrophe. I'd never had a garden. I knew absolutely nothing about it, but with a small rented cottage for the summer I woke up one fine morning and decided to have a garden. Anybody, I told myself, should be able to grow lettuce and radishes and onions. And flowers. Seeds sprout and flowers grow, don't they?

One side of the house (the north side) looked like a pretty place for a flower bed. Down the slope past a child's sandbox there was an empty window box on a small garage. At the other side of the lawn, almost a hundred yards from the cottage, was the place for my salad garden. I had the plot dug up and it was about the size of a 9' by 12' rug.

I went to the grocery store in the nearest village. I looked over the rack of seed packets and chose radishes, onions, lettuce (it was loose leaf). Then I saw a packet of New Zealand spinach. I'd never heard of New Zealand spinach but I liked spinach so I added that. The flower packets were harder to decide on. The pictures on the front all looked so entrancing. I finally picked a packet of mixed flower seeds, and also one of asters, one of Portulaca and, because I like them, forget-me-nots. Deep blue.

I planted my vegetable garden first in that tiny plot. Neat rows of lettuce and radish and onion seeds. Rows much too close and all of the seed planted at the same time. The New Zealand spinach packet had directions that baffled me. "Plant in hills," they said, "about four feet apart." So I heaped up hills four feet apart about two feet high and planted the spinach seeds all up and down the sides.

For my flower bed I had to scratch through that combination of loose soil and gobs of stucco that seems so often to surround a new house. I scratched, scattered the flower seeds indiscriminately, and covered them according to directions. Then I hurried down the sloping lawn to plant the window box at the small garage. Nothing ever happened in that window box, but along my path, in the sandbox, and in any bare spots on the lawn, beautiful red and yellow and pink Portulaca bloomed. Wherever my open seed packet had spilled a few seeds. That's when I learned that Portulaca prefers sun and sandy soil and doesn't have to be coddled.

When the first green shoots appeared in my flower garden beside the house, I was completely baffled. Which were flowers and which were weeds? I phoned a friend who lived ten miles away. Madeline had a beautiful formal garden—*and* a gardener. I told her my problem. She came right over, took one look, and knelt down and began to pluck out weeds as I tried to remember what weeds looked like. After a few minutes she said, "What kind of flowers did you plant?" I told her about the flower mixture and the asters and Portulaca and Chinese forget-me-nots. She was most tactful. "Asters are pretty hard to grow," she said gently, looking at the soil and the northern exposure. "Some of the mixed flowers should do all right—cosmos, Calendula, candytuft, cornflowers—but I don't know about Chinese forget-me-nots."

The Chinese forget-me-nots were superb. I've never been able to duplicate them for height or bloom. In fact, a neighbor child asked me for a bouquet of them for Flower Day at school, and we won first prize. The only other things that bloomed were spindly cornflowers and tall weak-stemmed Calendula and coreopsis which tried to tower to reach the light above the forget-me-nots. But I'll always bless Madeline for not discouraging my first garden attempt. I had flowers! But I did learn that the north side of a house is not the best place for a flower garden. And I learned to plant unknown flower seed in rows.

The small vegetable garden seemed to be a complete success. The leaf lettuce was young and tender. I picked some at its early stage, sliced radishes and tiny scallions all paper thin, added French dressing, and discovered a delicious salad. But one day when I went out to pick a salad I found that a rabbit had nibbled all the lettuce to the ground. I was heartbroken. Until I saw a few days later that new tender lettuce had started growing again from the roots. The rabbit came back from time to time and nibbled away, and I had young tender lettuce all summer. I learned that all lettuce, loose-leaf or head lettuce, can be cut down to ground level and will regrow from the crown.

The New Zealand spinach throve. I did have to go out and build up the hills again every time it rained. It rained a lot that summer and the hills got pretty muddy, and so did I. Then Russell, a knowledgeable gardener, came for a visit and I proudly showed him my vegetable garden. He took one look at my spinach and tried

to control his laughter. "What," he finally asked, "are the Indian burial mounds for?" I told him what the seed packet had said, "Plant in hills." And he patiently explained to me that "hills" doesn't mean hills. It means planting several seeds close together just below ground level, then thinning them out when the plants appear and leaving only the strongest.

After that summer I knew gardening was for me. Just look at the vegetables I'd grown! Look at the flowers! Look how easy it was!

THE ROCKY GARDEN

My next garden showed me that it wasn't that easy and that I still had a great deal to learn. Another house in the country, and this time a garden over half a mile away. Not really a garden, but a plot of ground to be made into a garden. Morning after morning I walked up that hill and worked happily six hours a day, trying to tame that soil. Broiling sun and rocky soil that had to be attacked with a mattock. I used that mattock until bursitis set in. Then, one arm in a sling, I planted with the other arm.

That was the year I planted my first row of corn. And learned that corn is not bee pollinated, it is wind pollinated and each row has to be backed up by another row. I had beautiful corn stalks, but few kernels on the ears. I also learned that corn seed can be planted between rocks, that anything that grows up doesn't need deep-rooted soil. And that things that grow down, like root vegetables, will grow among the rocks if you first thrust down a pointed stick, open a hole, fill it with soil and then plant your seed. Root crops need room to grow their roots.

Then I found better soil on that land, beyond the rocky ledge. It was a strange looking crazy-quilt garden, but it produced vegetables. And I canned, how I canned! I was a novice at canning but wartime rationing was on, all vegetables were gold for the growing, and I knew that limas—all beans—were precious protein. I felt both virtuous and patriotic as I canned my harvest. A good deal of what I canned spoiled, and that which didn't spoil hadn't much flavor. But I learned. And the summer squash I canned was fine. I cooked it, put it through a kitchen sieve, and had essence of summer squash to which I added milk for soup.

That garden was my first laboratory. There was no water except at a small hand pump, and it was a dry summer. In a way that was fortunate, for I learned that a little water is a dangerous thing, and it is better to hoe up soil around the plants and aerate them. I still use that system.

I worked that garden for several years and remember it gratefully. There I learned to have the soil limed, manured, plowed, and harrowed each spring. With that done, all I had to do was to rake and plant—and pick up stones. I learned that one small boy can be a great help in weeding or picking up stones, but that two boys are no help at all.

It was in that garden that I got a top accolade from Fred and Esther, friends and professional gardeners with a greenhouse. They stopped by to bring me a magnificent head of lettuce, grown in their greenhouse, which I had not yet learned to grow. Looking about my garden, they exclaimed at my yellow summer squash plants which were huge and bore profusely. How, they asked, had I grown such mammoth plants? I explained that I had simply dug a big deep hole, put fertilizer in the bottom, filled up the hole with soil, and planted the squash seed. Indians buried fish under their corn, beans and squash, and I figured that since I didn't have any fish I would try fertilizer. Fred, then editor of the garden page of the *New York Times*, tried, with Esther, to cram some more knowledge in me. But they knew that a beginning gardener, no matter how ardent, must learn by experiment, trial, and error.

THE TOMATO-PATCH
GARDEN

My next garden was a tomato patch, nothing else. It was a strip of old, worn-out grass near the house, convenient to tend and easy to harvest. There's no enjoyment in carrying a heavy load of tomatoes half a mile from garden to kitchen. So I had the old grass strip plowed and it provided my third experience, this time with new fresh-turned sod, good soil, and no stones.

The tomato patch was easy to put in. The soil was rich and the plants grew and sprawled with lots of room. I have never seen such tomatoes! Sun-red, red-ripe, full of sun, air, and rain. And plenty of room. I still prefer sprawled tomatoes to any method where tomatoes are confined. But stakes and poles are fine, and what gardener has room enough to let tomatoes take over a whole garden?

On the north side of that house a short way from my sun-ripening tomatoes was a shady wooded area. I spied some wild strawberries and immediately started to pick them, eating some as I picked. Strawberry jam, I thought to myself, and how wonderful that would be come winter. The strawberry jam spoiled. And there was poison ivy all around the strawberry plants, and I still didn't know poison ivy leaves. So I kept yellow laundry soap and rubbing alcohol handy every time after I picked more wild strawberries. But I made a discovery! A tall yellow daisy was growing there and it looked so pretty that I picked it. With it up came a misshapen tuberlike root, like an awkward potato. I looked in every garden encyclopedia I could find, and finally came upon what it was. A Jerusalem artichoke. I knew the globe artichoke well, but I'd never seen a Jerusalem artichoke. I experimented with cooking some of the tubers and found that paring the skins is practically impossible. But if you put the tubers into hot boiling water, then take them out almost immediately, the skins will slip right off. And if they are not overcooked—which is the danger point—they are delicious served with hollandaise sauce or just butter. They can even be frozen. Freezing was still unknown to me. But I certainly learned to watch for poison ivy.

THE PREPLANTED GARDEN

My next garden was with a rented house. (How we all move around.) A rented house with a beautiful, spacious green lawn and a garden already planted. Beyond the spacious green lawn and flowerbeds and outside the garden were vines with winter squash and pumpkins trailing out from under the birch and beech trees. One vine to a tree. I can see now that a few seeds planted under a tree, then thinned to one strong vine, would trail out and travel away from the shade to get sunshine and air. I tried this technique later with winter squash and pumpkin, letting them trail over the weedy edges of a garden. One vine only. And if it trails up a fence at an edge of a garden, you can always find the gold of a pumpkin or a winter squash.

THE HILLTOP GARDEN

After that came the garden with the best soil I have ever seen. It came with the hilltop house we bought. There was almost half an acre of deep brown fertile soil at the foot of the hill, silt-washed without a pebble in it, enriched with the mixture of topsoil from the hill and chicken manure from an old abandoned shack of a chicken house some ways from the house. So big a garden that I could plant anything I wanted. No problem of space. It was a gardener's paradise. The man who plowed it for me said it was the best soil he had ever turned. After he had harrowed it it didn't need anything except to be planted—it was so fine and mellow.

But it was at the bottom of the hill—and oh that hill! It was as steep as an alp. I'd set out from the hilltop house with seeds, garden tools, face tissues, a vacuum bottle of water and a sweat-wipe towel. But if I'd forgotten anything I found myself looking up at that hill and wishing I were a mountain goat, able to jump from crag to crag. It wasn't very far down, but it was a long, long way up and the hill got steeper every time I climbed it. Going down was easy. Coming up I was loaded with everything I'd taken down, and eventually with vegetables too. And tired from gardening.

The second year of working that beautiful garden made me think twice about the trip down and up. I needed a kitchen garden. A tiny garden right near the house and the kitchen where I could run out and pick a sprig of parsley or a cucumber or some lettuce, not go down that hill for a scallion, for instance. So Hal ripped out a small rose bed near the house and transplanted the roses. (We had other rose beds—enough roses to fulfill a long-time dream of mine of having enough roses for every room in the house.) I planted radishes, a climbing cucumber, lettuce, parsley, scallions. Handy to my kitchen. The main garden flourished down below, and it was a comfortable feeling to know it was growing away, awaiting planned excursions.

The big garden had such an abundance of yield that I blithely agreed to sell the surplus to a friend's tenant farmer who had a roadside vegetable stand. Hal and I couldn't possibly eat up all those squash and cucumbers and peas and corn, and I had lost interest in canning. And right there and then I found out that I would never again sell anything from my garden. All the fun went out of it. It was nature's bounty, not mine, and could not be translated into terms of cash. It is one of the most valuable lessons I have ever learned and I have never forgotten it. My garden was for eating or giving away.

MY FAVORITE GARDEN

When we bought the Salisbury house in the lower Berkshires I thought, Here is my ideal garden. Here I can put to use all the knowledge I have gained in all those other gardens. You don't buy a house for a garden, but if the perfect garden comes with the house, what more could any gardener want?

The garden was about 100' by 100' square. It was fenced. On level ground. Handy to the house. Lighter soil than in the Hilltop Garden. Not a stone in it. If I wanted to squash a bug I had to go outside the garden to find a couple of stones. There were two gates, one to go into the garden, and another wide one on the roadside, wide enough when it was unbarred to allow a tractor or a manure spreader in.

We had bought the farmhouse, with its acres of fields and pasture land and one side of a wooded mountain, in a dairy-farming valley. Cows, alfalfa, field corn, hay, milk trucks, and neighbors half a mile apart.

Sandra and Ricky who had preceded us and from whom we bought our house and land were weekenders. City people. Sandra had planted beautiful and expensive shrubbery all around the house, and beautiful and expensive perennial flowers and a rock garden outside the vegetable-garden gate. While we were waiting for our furniture to arrive, Ricky, who was obviously in charge of the vegetable garden, took me out to see it. There was a splendid row of strawberries, a little Swiss chard, but to my amazement I saw a long row of beets practically bulging out of the soil. I asked why they hadn't eaten them. I will never forget his answer. He said, "Oh, they were all such different sizes that every time I brought some into the house the cook said she didn't know how to cook them."

I was a little glad that Ricky did not know much about beets and that the cook did not know how to cook them. I expected those beets to be woody—they were so big. But they were delicious, and we feasted.

Hal insisted that I planted lettuce seed before our furniture

arrived. A canard, of course. Because I do not normally carry seed packets in my pockets. And all my seeds were with the furniture. Probably I planted lettuce the next day.

On the afternoon that we arrived to take possession of our new house, I had noticed a flourishing vegetable garden down the road. On a farmer's front lawn! I was fascinated. So after we had our furniture somewhat settled in we went down to see Albert who owned that garden and had been renting our fields for hay and pasturing his cows. I said I was a gardener and wondered what kind of seeds he planted. He turned to me and nodded tolerantly and resumed his conversation with Hal about alfalfa, corn, and other field crops. I broke in again, asking "When do you have early frost and late frost?" He said, "Well, one summer we had frost every month. I thought you said you were a gardener." And turned back to Hal. Man talk. I could just feel him thinking "City people again." I flounced—at least mentally I flounced—over to look at his garden. It was about 50' by 100'. There were long rows of radishes, head lettuce, cabbage, carrots, beets, a double row of corn, squashes, cucumbers. Nothing fenced in, but everything where he could keep an eye on it right from his house. His wife, Ruth, later told me that Albert planted enough for the whole town.

So I went about garden planting in my usual way. My lettuce bed. My cabbage bed. Thinking, "All right, so I'm just a city girl." But I began to notice that when I was out in the garden working, Albert, on his tractor haying our land or getting a recalcitrant cow home, would come close to my garden and would look over somewhat surreptitiously.

Then he began to watch the way I waited for a rain so I could transplant. Then he finally asked how I managed to get head lettuce in the middle of hot August. I explained my way, and from then on Albert would appear with a flat and a trowel when it was raining heavily and ask if he could have a few transplants from my garden.

I felt quite triumphant. He looked at my part rows, instead of the long rows he had been planting, and he began to plant his the same way. We even had a bet on every summer as to who would get the first yellow summer squash. He always won. But I swear that he started his in the house.

So we had Albert the farmer-down-the-road, and Charlie the farmer-up-the-road. Both of them came to know my gardening zest, and one of them every year saw to it that my garden was manured, plowed, and harrowed without my even asking. Dairy farmers both. Good neighbors. Charlie had a small kitchen garden and began to plant in part rows too. His wife, Letha, said to me one day, "How can you stand that smell of manure!" I said, "I love the smell of manure. Because once my garden has been manured I know that pretty soon I can start planting."

I definitely expected that this new, almost perfect garden that I had would take care of all my earlier mistakes, and that I knew enough to handle all of them. I was mistaken. I found out that a gardener is always learning. I don't think a gardener ever stops learning. Trial and error again. But perhaps that is the fun of gardening. That you never really learn it all. And you keep on learning.

One week I had the odd experience of one person saying to me "What a small garden," and another person saying "What a big garden." The first was a farm woman who had learned that we had horse-radish roots to spare. (I think she brought her whole family.) Farmers think in terms of yield. Quantity, not quality. Whereas I think in terms of young vegetables for flavor and texture.

There was horse-radish in the perennial flower bed and also in the vegetable garden. Hal and I tried grating some of the root in the kitchen. Once was enough. After that we grated our horse-radish out in the back yard, and found that even scraps of the root take hold and grow. But the horse-radish leaves of that tremendous plant are a delicacy when minced in a salad.

The man who takes care of our typewriters arrived that same week. Before he left, he asked if he might look at my garden. I went out with him and he said "What a big garden." He had just started his first vegetable garden in his small back yard and marveled at mine, while I glowed, as any gardener would. He fired questions at me and I tried to answer them, recalling my First Garden, knowing you have to learn a garden.

"Would your methods work anywhere?" he finally asked.

That was a poser. I thought of the lush black mucklands of Florida's truck-garden area, the fertile valleys of Colorado and southwestern Utah and northern Idaho, the irrigated lands of California and Nevada, even Maine with its short summers.

"I think so. Depending on soil, weather conditions and climate. But I've only gardened in lower and upper Connecticut and lower New York State."

I finally figured it out. Small garden or big garden, it's all in your point of view.

As for me, I was beginning to wish I had more room to try more new vegetables. A gardener never has enough room, or thinks he hasn't. My garden started to feel cramped as I juggled for space. I began to look yearningly at a long strip of land on the other side of the house, beyond the gnarled old apple trees and lilacs in our dooryard, where there had been a chicken run. (The year we moved in we reclaimed the chicken house, which had a cement floor. One side of it made a workshop for Hal's power tools. The other side had enough room for a Ping-Pong table. In cleaning out the chicken house we had shoveled out layers of well-rotted chicken manure onto the old chicken run. Remembering the terrific soil at the Hilltop Garden, I decided this would be just what I wanted, with priceless nitrogen.)

I planned it would be just plowed, not fenced, and I began to think in terms of what vegetables woodchucks and rabbits wouldn't care about, at least not too much, compared to my main garden. I planted carrots, beets, succession corn, parsnips, and melons. The corn did fine. All root crops were a failure. The chickweed, or whatever you call it, throve. Too *much* nitrogen in the soil. Too *much* chicken fertilizer.

When harvest came, I found myself lugging dishpans full of heavy vegetables back and forth, till I felt like the Sorcerer's Apprentice. A few dozen ears of corn, unshucked, is quite a few trips. And that summer was the one with a drought and the succession corn came all at the same time. Melons are heavy carrying. But the worst of all was that every time I reached for a hoe or any tool, it was in the other garden. I settled happily for my one garden. I knew my one garden. But I did learn about differing soil, even on the same land.

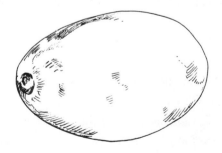

A GARDENER'S HOLIDAY

In order to have a lazy, luxurious garden season with only three half
hours a week needed for care and tending I finally learned that two
heavy planting days are necessary, one when the vegetables that can
take frost are put in, and the second when the main garden is planted
with the tender crops after all frost danger is over. And, oh! How
those unused winter-weary muscles creak and groan until a hot tub
or shower takes care of them.

But seeds would be in the ground, not yelling at me, "Get me
in the ground! Any old which-way! Just get me in the ground!" I
never like seeds pushing *at* me—or being a slave to a garden when
it's summertime and I have a million other things I want to do.

Then I learned, with my Salisbury Garden, the most splendid
timesaver of all. To plan and chart my garden in the winter. And I
wondered why it had never occurred to me before. A week off in
winter—sort of a Gardener's Holiday. Of course it doesn't take a
week to plan and chart my next summer's garden. But I prolong it,
just to think and feel gardening. In winter! With no worry about
bugs, mosquitoes, blight, heat, drought. No worry about weather,
frost, climate, just delighting in visualizing the garden, as I measure
the height of plants and their position. Of course I must also measure the height and position of plants in the garden itself, but that is
for later.

As soon as the seed catalogues begin to roll in I put them aside,
vowing to myself that I will not look at those alluring "new" discov-
eries—those glamourous new promises, in color—until I have charted
out my own "musts" that I know I will want.

My winter planning method goes like this. I get out everything
I am going to need for my charting. (Just as I get out all ingredients
before I cook a recipe.) Pencils sharpened, an emery board to clean

pencil erasers, paper, a ruler, a yardstick and a tape measure, last year's notes to myself, "Don't get again," "Get more of," "Was wonderful," "Was terrible."

There will be two identical charts on paper when I have finished. One will be the can-get-grimy one that can go into the garden, and a clean chart that I will keep in the house for notes to myself. This may sound complicated, but it really isn't.

I start by drawing a path down the middle of both sheets. That path will be mowed all summer, to prevent any possible gullies in a rain that might wash out my vegetable plants. Next, I divide the two sides of the chart. On each side will be planted my part rows of vegetables.

Every garden has its boundaries. So I rough in the far roadside end where that sometimes flowing brook will be dried up during gardening season. On the right end of this garden I must rough in an oblong for the asparagus bed. I know where the lettuce seedbeds will go, on the upper right-hand side of the path just inside the garden gate, a wet area that I never change because the lettuce likes it there. Then I must mark out space for the rotation of corn and tomatoes. This side last year, the other side this year. The herb garden will be marked on the upper left-hand side of the path. And because I like a row of cutting annuals in my vegetable garden for pretty, that row must be just beyond the herbs or that beautiful machinery will not have room to get in the roadside gate.

Space. At this point I always get stumped. I am going to have to allow space on my chart for vegetables that need a whole season's growing. Lima beans, corn, tomatoes, New Zealand spinach, parsnips, leeks (if I decide I want them), also transplanted cabbages, pole beans twining up giant sunflowers, Italian flat beans, summer squash, pepper plants, and so on.

It all begins to seem like a very small garden. I know the winter squash and pumpkin can travel to its edges. Also any melons or

FLOWING BROOK

RHUBARB

SUNFLOWERS and POLE BEANS

TINY TOMATOES to RESEED

MAIN TOMATO PATCH

MAIN TOMATO PATCH

CABBAGE SEED BED

CABBAGE TRANSPLANTS

NEW ZEALAND SPINACH

ONION SEED BED

FLOWERS

HERBS

TRAILING VINES

WINTER SQUASH

PUMPKINS

MELONS

ASPARAGUS

LIMA BEANS (BUSH)

PEAS

CORN

PEAS

PEPPER ZUCCHINI PEPPER ZUCCHINI PEPPER ZUCCHINI

SNAP BEANS

CARROTS

BEETS

ONION SETS
ONION SETS

EGGPLANTS

BEETS, WAX BEANS
SNAP BEANS CARROTS

YELLOW SQUASH

LETTUCE SEED BED

PATTY PAN SQUASH (WHITE)

GARDEN GATE

watermelons. (I have never found one baby watermelon that was worth the bother.)

But I have now marked on my duplicate charts Garden gate, My gate, at the top of the charts. (Instead of North, South, West, East, as that is too confusing when I go out to the garden with my seed packets and garden paraphernalia.) There is my 100' by 100' garden. And I have my chart to follow.

One year I decided not to make a chart. After all, didn't I know this garden by heart? And my ways of planting? No. I enlisted Hal's help to mark the path and the side rows with the twine and sticks. And I found myself utterly paralyzed as to what to put where. As Hal stood patiently waiting, string and marker ready, he would say "Where do you want this row?" And I, wandering in some far corner of the garden, would say, "I don't know. I have to think."

From then on, I did my winter charting. It was a bad year for the uncharted garden. The corn overshadowed all its neighboring small crops. Parsnips, carrots, even beets, were stunted by the towering corn stalks. You can do what you want with your garden. But I advise knowing in winter what you want and where.

My next discovery was completely unexpected. There was a church auction. A baby's wicker "dresserette" was up for bidding. I started to bid. Hal whispered to me, "What in thunder do you want that thing for?" I whispered back, "Shh! For my seeds." I got it for two dollars. The flat top opens up. The drawers open sideways. It stands on four legs. It can be closed up tight. Seed packets can be stowed away all winter, and neither mice nor dust will get into it when closed up.

I used to scurry around the house at planting time, trying to collect all the garden paraphernalia I needed. Such a waste of time. Then I found that I could keep in the top of the dresserette such things as bandanas, insect repellant, meat tenderizer (with enzymes that work on bites), Ace ankle bandages if I needed them, summer socks, suntan lotion, Vaseline sticks for chapped lips, coils of paper-covered wire twist ties, packets of face tissue, paperclips for opened seed packets, and this season's garden notes. The drawers will hold boxes of all shapes and kinds in which to keep any leftover seed packets. No more hurrying around to collect things I might need when the garden is calling. That two dollars proved a priceless investment!

Now I can look at those seed catalogues. See what they are trying to sell me this year. Having planned and made my garden charts of my old favorites first, I can feel somewhat impervious to their claims. I don't want their startling new hybrids. I know I will be ordering five or six kinds of carrots. I know that I will be getting eight or nine varieties of lettuce. I know that I will be getting several varieties of beets. Yellow squash, white scalloped patty pan, and zucchini, from slim marrow to regular green and the enormous black. Cucumbers, a pickling variety. And with any luck at all I'll be finding some of every vegetable that has always done well.

Flower deciding will be the cherry on top of the sundae, after my serious—or somewhat serious—business of vegetables is done. After all, I am ordering vegetable seeds for year-round eating and freezing. Therefore it's of special importance.

By now, even if there is two feet of snow on the ground I am practically eating out of that garden.

Now I can make out my seed order. Why do I always put "Please Rush!" at the top of the orders? I'm sure it doesn't hurry them one bit. Is it my urgency to have the seeds come in? To hope, "Well, we might have an early spring"?

TIPS AND TOOLS

WEEDS

I use weeds. Weeds are essential to my way of gardening. They are a necessity for every vegetable I grow. Mine is not a show garden and if anyone points proudly to a garden that has no weeds in it, I keep quiet. But I am thinking, "My way of gardening is so much easier. I don't care how many weeds grow between vegetable rows; it's those rows of vegetables that matter to me."

MULCHES

I have tried mulches, but because my basic method is hoe-up-the-dirt, I quickly abandoned them. You can't hoe up black plastic or hulls or any kind of mulch.

CROP ROTATION

I found that the simplest way to handle this was to plant in part rows, and when that particular crop was finished, just to pull it out and replant a different vegetable. It seems to make for a natural rotation.

WATER

I never use water except for transplanting. Even then, I prefer a soaking rain. We have a faucet on the side of the house nearest the garden and long lengths of hose for emergency use only, but we seldom needed to use it even in a severe drought, because way below surface level you can usually find water to hoe up around plants.

SPRAYS

I will never use poison sprays. I will only use pure rotenone dust, which can easily be rinsed off. Let the flowers go to pieces or the tomatoes or the potatoes get blight and be finished, I say, but only rotenone will they get. I refuse to eat poison.

HYBRIDS I've learned to be wary of hybrids. After you've gardened for many years you learn to know which seeds you can count on. I've found most hybrid seed may grow better, but a lot of the original flavor has been hybridized out.

COMPOST I knew nothing about compost heaps. Automatically, as a gardener, I had thrown carrot thinnings and old beet tops and onion tops back on the ground every time I thinned or pulled out vegetables, figuring that the following year they would be a fine thing when my garden was plowed again. Then it seemed a rather disorderly way, so a boarded compost heap was made in back of the woodshed, to which we added garbage, till we found that every dog within a mile of us visited that compost daily. And it took time to go out the garden gate to the back of the woodshed. So I started a compost heap inside the garden gate. Then Hal put boards around it. Much easier. Just toss the finished pea vines or thinning tops there. But I learned never to throw a bug-eaten vine or root in. Those were for burning.

Just over the fence from the compost heap, a pear tree grew in the perennial border. The ripened fruits dropped into it. Good compost.

While we were using the back-of-the-woodshed compost we noticed one strange thing. Some old sprouting potatoes took root one year and we had marvelous potato vines. And potatoes. Evidently neither dogs nor any wildlife likes potatoes. Too fattening? Or no interest in car-

bohydrates? Let a veterinarian or a vitamin spe-
cialist figure out that one.

Two sneakered feet and two hands are my
most important tools. And the quickest. When
it's sifting soil through my fingers to cover tiny
seed, it's my fingers. (I've tried to wear gloves and
given up on them. My ungloved fingers are more
sensitive in calculating the amount of soil I need.
If you remember to run your fingernails through a
bar of soap before gardening, your nails will thank
you.) My two sneakered feet are for tamping down
the soil firmly after I plant any seeds. Why bother
to find a flat-bottomed tool when your feet do a
better job?

Because of my hoe-up method of gardening,
a hoe is vitally important. I prefer a long-handled
heart-shaped (triangular) hoe. A regular hoe can
be used, but I advise a narrow-headed one, to avoid
damage to the growing roots, when it is necessary
to hoe up soil between the double rows or at the
sides. I use a long-handled four-fingered rake to
scratch through lettuce or cabbage beds if the germination is too thick. I see to it that I have a
steel-toothed rake for use if the soil gets caked.
Two trowels are usually needed. One very narrow
one and one wider one. (Any hand tools are worth
the price if they are made of aluminum. They will
last for years and never get rusty.)

I keep all of the tools in a basket near the
edge of the garden gate, to remind me to put tools
in it before I quit gardening. Any kind of porous

basket, so an unexpected rain will allow drainage. It's a big help at harvest time when you put the garden to bed for the winter to know where to find your tools, and to put some kind of oil from the kitchen on them to avoid rust forming through the winter.

I am purposely avoiding kitchen knives in tools. I long ago decided that instead of handing out a small knife to some friend with instructions to cut off a squash or a tomato half-an-inch above the stem (for better keeping) and adding "Bring back the knife," it was wiser for me to do the picking. I wonder how many small paring knives will eventually turn up in my garden!

MARKERS

Fancy markers for rows and varieties of vegetables can be bought. I find it simpler to have a batch of sticks at the edge of the garden to mark planted rows, until the vegetables are tall enough to proclaim what they are. Then I put the sticks back in the basket at the edge of the garden till their next use. At picking time, jagged sticks can get in your way.

SIDE DRESSING

Fertilizer (such as dried sheep manure, dried cow manure, dried chicken manure, or any commercial fertilizer) diluted with water or a welcome rain, is used by many gardeners around plants, in the hope that it will add vigor and vitality to the crop. I never use it because it is too apt to burn the roots of plants.

SOIL TESTING

I always thought I should have my garden soil tested. But I never did. It seemed unnecessary

even when I thought of those fascinating little
kits that you can buy to tell you the proportions
of lime, nitrogen, etc. The garden yield came out
so splendidly merely by rotation of the crops I
planted. And my method of pulling out a crop
once its yield is over and replanting a different
crop.

CLOTHES   Dress for your job. Before I knew much about
gardening I knew a lady gardener who used to
bring me some of her choice vegetables. Garden
fresh. She wore a lovely summer frock, a broad-
brimmed hat, and carried a long-handled basket
that turned down at the sides, in which she carried pretty, colorful vegetables. How I admired
her and her gardening clothes. She always
reminded me of one of those Christmas catalogues with the mother, beautifully dressed in a
beautiful negligee, accompanied by two children
in equally dainty clothes, descending the curving
stairway to view the pictured Christmas tree in
the livingroom.

It never happened to me. Nor have I ever
dressed for gardening like Lady Bountiful. Me, I
had three pairs of blue jeans. Inside the waist-
bands I made my own Zip Code. In red floss was
"G" for "gardening" on one, "F" for "fishing" on
another, and the third was a larger size for muddy,
rainy days. Several pairs of sneakers, light-weight
to heavy-soled can-get-muddy to go with my worst
beat-up jeans, long-sleeved cotton and flannel-
ette shirts I stole from Hal, an old fedora (also

stolen). Rainy-day garb. For transplanting. Sunny days, bib overalls or khaki shorts and a halter or summer blouse, and bandannas tied around my hair, and lightweight sneakers. I never achieved Lady Bountiful, but how my garden grew! After all, a gardener has to be comfortable. And clothes a couple of sizes too big mean more comfort. Pockets, pockets, pockets! A gardener has to have pockets.

CONDITIONING   To my utter amazement, I began to find out that my gardening had fringe benefits. I would acquire a grand suntan while gardening on sunny days. Of course I might have to shift a halter to get an even tan. Simple enough, I found. And better than lying on a beach, where you once again have to adjust straps and halters, where you do nothing but lie in the sun and keep turning. It seemed to prove that if you are doing something you love to do, you become so interested that you forget any of it is work. Exercising muscles, strengthening your whole body, flattening your tummy muscles and that middle-age spread. I give it to you for what it's worth.

GLAMOUR   How not to be a wallflower. Most women prefer flower gardening. Most men, if they garden at all, are vegetable gardeners. You might wish you were that woman who seems to be in animated conversation with several men talking to her, equally animated, and wonder what they are talking about. They are probably discussing how big their radishes were this year, or what new variety of corn they are planting, or what type of

blight is hitting their tomatoes. Vegetable gardeners are so generous, exchanging ideas and their
experiences. Don't stand on the sidelines won-
dering "What has she got that I haven't got?"
Answer: Vegetable gardening.

Part 2

WAYS WITH VEGETABLES

$\mathcal{I}$ am a wayward, willful, contrary gardener. I don't follow seed-packet directions. I find my methods of short cuts and timesavers so much easier.

Seed packet directions say to plant thin. I plant thick. Thinning is easy, and by planting thick I prevent unsightly gaps. If seedlings come up close together it doesn't matter. And what have I to lose but a few seeds?

I have found that in a good summer all-day rain, many vegetables can be moved to a different spot in their same row, settle in, and never know that they have been moved at all—bush beans, bush limas, and pole beans if not more than five or six inches tall, and corn no more than ten inches tall if the seed is still attached to it and it is moved and replanted the same rainy day. Neighbors without corn in their gardens are always delighted to have the corn seedlings to plant.

When I was doing newspaper columns about gardening, the editor of the garden page phoned me and said, "Your column this week says that you have no weeds in your tall corn."

"I don't," I told him.

"It's impossible," he said, "and we have to go to press today."

"But it's true," I said indignantly. "Do you want me to go out and look?"

"Please do."

I skipped out to check my sweet corn. Not a weed. "It's my

hoe-up method," I tried to explain. He ran the column, but I could feel he was still dubious. He was puzzled. But it was true.

I plant most seed in part or third rows. Sometimes only a yard long. I think that because of my way of planting seed in part rows and pulling out a crop once its heaviest yield is done, I have avoided many a bug or blight situation that most gardeners contend with. And then I plant seeds of a different variety in that row. So my Salisbury Garden always has tiny, flavorful crops at hand for my special delight.

I rarely save seeds from my garden. The one time I wish I had was from the Hilltop Garden, when I had a special variety of climbing cucumbers against the wall where we took out the roses and Hal transplanted them. The following year I ordered more. "Sorry. We have no seed," was the reply. Ouch!

I always keep any leftover seed for the following year of beans, carrots, beets, the lettuce family, all the cabbage family, squash (summer and winter), radishes, New Zealand spinach, cucumbers, and peas. These will hold over and may surprise you utterly at planting time. As good as new. And sometimes better.

I throw out leftover onion, parsley, and parsnip seed. I won't chance those the following year.

I have tried to include the basic vegetables that a novice gar-

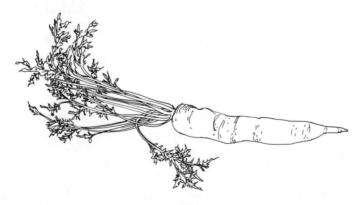

dener, or even a pro, is apt to plant, but I may mention some other vegetables along the way. Who wants to bother with salsify (oyster plant), celery, okra, leeks, white turnips, rutabagas, eggplant, wit-loof chicory, endive, or escarole—which mean extra weeding and extra work—unless the gardener wants to experiment or include vegetables the family particularly likes. There are many splendid garden encyclopedias and vegetable gardening books that can be turned to (as I have often done) for reference.

BUSH   BEANS

I always plant green bush beans (I still call them "string beans") in a double row instead of a single row. A double row saves garden space, gives twice the yield of a single row, cuts in half the time spent planting and tending and rotenoning. But, most important of all, each row acts as backstop for the other row so they can lean across towards each other for protection against wind or heavy rain which might weaken the plants and loosen the roots.

To plant bush beans, I set my marker string as for any other single row. Then I make two furrows for my part rows, two to three inches deep and about nine or ten inches apart, one on each side of the marker string. I strew seeds very thickly in each furrow, cover with soil and tamp down very firmly. Those bean seeds are apt to push up through the soil before they sprout, so I want hard-packed soil covering them or else I may have to go out to the garden and push any exposed beans back into the ground, especially after a rain.

I used to think all beans must be planted carefully, one by one, spaced just so. It's unnecessary. But strew plenty of seed. Two plants can come quite close together because those plants are going to full out above ground, some may not develop and some may be bird-nipped or frost-nipped.

Cultivation of the double row is easy. When the plants are a few inches high and the inevitable weeds start up between and at the sides of the rows, just take a hoe and pull it down the middle of that double row, heaping both soil and weeds against the plants. Do this same hoeing-up on the outer side of each row. The heart-shaped hoe is the best tool I have found for this because its curved edges will throw up soil against the roots of the plants without any possible cutting of the roots. But any hoe will do if you are very careful not to damage the roots. Then forget the weeds. From then on, any weeds will provide extra moisture and support. At picking time I may pull out some of the German weed, grasses, or any tall weeds for my own convenience in gathering beans. By then the roots of the plants are strong enough so that pulling any weeds will not matter.

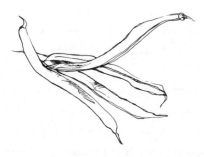

The Mexican bean beetle is the constant enemy of beans and must be watched for carefully. It is a yellow-and-black chewing beetle that lays a yellow mass of eggs on the undersides of the leaves—but don't confuse it with the ladybug that looks somewhat similar but is a friend to a garden. Dusting with rotenone may be necessary, and if you see one Mexican beetle on the leaves and then find the egg mass under a leaf, rotenone heavily under the leaves and throughout the plants, and when you pull out those plants carry them far away from the garden to dry or be burned, but never added to a compost heap.

The big yield of bush beans comes at one certain stage of the bush-bean plants. That yield will be tremendous. But bush beans must never be picked when wet, because rust or blight may develop. So if rain threatens, I dash out to the garden and grab every bean that can be picked, so I will be sure to have beans for the eating. After the big yield I pull those bean plants out.

The first tiny beans, almost with the blossom still on, seem like an unbelievable treat. Later, the mature beans have their own extraordinary flavor.

I always plant a few yellow wax beans at the far end of each part row of green bush beans. When the green and yellow beans are young, they can be cooked whole together and have a similar taste. The mature beans call for a longer cooking time. The mature green beans, tipped and cut, when cooked in boiling salted water, reach a stage that is woody. Test and taste. They may need five minutes more of cooking to make them tender.

Mature wax beans have a distinct flavor when cut into quarter-inch pieces and cooked in boiling salted water. They take much longer to cook than green beans, but they are worth the effort.

Every vegetable gardener is constantly delighted at the different taste of each vegetable from the garden. It's brand-new and seems wonderful.

Hal and I always marveled at the different flavor of each garden vegetable that I gathered and brought into the kitchen, even to having a small dish of that fresh taste any time of day or for a whole luncheon or supper.

As to varieties, I will plant only round-podded beans. All flat-podded beans tend to be watery, mushy, and tasteless. Markets usually carry mainly the flat-podded beans because they look prettier and keep better while the round-podded bean shows its age by getting brownish and tired-looking. Not for my garden.

A delicious combination can be made with green bush beans and mushrooms, if you sauté a few sliced mushrooms in butter and then add to them your cooked green bush beans.

LIMA   BEANS

If you like limas as much as I like limas they will be a "must" for your garden. I prefer bush limas. I have tried pole limas in every way I can think of. I have always ended up with beautiful vines but only a few pods of tiny measly beans. (However, Kentucky Wonders and Italian flat-podded green beans are a complete success.)

Limas need all season to mature, and require both planning and

space. So I devote a whole row to them. Two kinds of limas are always my choice—half of the row will hold the tiny buttery baby beans which give a tremendous yield at picking time. The other half of that row will be the large meatier beans that will be ready to pick after the prolific tiny ones have finished.

To plant, I again do double rows. I use my marker string and plant thick in two- to three-inch furrows, but the distance between the baby limas and the big limas differs because the size of the bush varies and the larger ones need more room. For the baby limas, about ten inches between furrows. For the larger bush limas, about a foot and a half. This much space is needed for the first weeding with a hoe between the double rows, and to hoe-up dirt on the outside of those rows to keep the weeds down as they first start up. I try to hoe-up more dirt at the outside of each row when I think of it. But I forget the weeds between the rows after that.

A fat juicy lima bean seems to be the special delight of all birds, who will even dig close to the ground surface to get them. And quite probably will leave holes in the row, if you haven't planted thick enough. It won't make any difference if two plants come up close together, and a young plant can always be moved on a rainy day if a sharp-beaked bird tries to get ahead of you.

Lima beans must be tamped down very firmly and often pushed back into the soil after a rain and before they sprout.

Lima beans are somewhat temperamental, and there is always the possibility that with too much rain they may rot in the soil without sprouting, so I usually find out if this is happening by using a thin trowel and digging up a spot in the row to make sure I am going to have limas. If the soil seems to have been too cold or too wet for sprouting I often plant another row right beside them, knowing they may be a later crop, but that I will be sure of having lima beans.

If the Mexican bean beetle attacks the limas it is not too serious because lima beans are shelled before eating, but rotenone dusting is wise from time to time to discourage any chewing or eating insect. And of course, any plant with yellow bean beetle egg masses on the undersides of leaves must never be thrown on the compost heap or left in the garden at cleanup time.

By the time the limas are ready to pick, many of the garden chores are over and many other crops finished. Limas are then a brand-new taste, worth the time spent picking and shelling. Because of the thick pod of a lima bean it is hard to tell when they are filled out. I try to pick them when I can see the bulges of the mature beans.

After waiting and watching limas all summer long, I cook them in my usual boiling method for green vegetables. Shell, boiling water ready, salt added, lid on, test and taste. About ten or fifteen minutes cooking time. Serve with butter and pepper added if desired. Usually that new taste of the end of the gardening season is so delicious that we gobble them right up. None left for freezing, but I attempt to save some for a casserole dish. This is my way with fresh green lima beans. Dried lima beans can be cooked alone or added to stews or soups. But we rarely have any leftover lima beans. Not fresh-from-the-garden green lima beans.

POLE BEANS

It seemed wonderful when I first learned that any kind of pole bean could be grown up twining around giant sunflowers. At first I planted in hills about four feet apart. Then I found that a single sunflower stalk can break off or be blown over in a heavy wind or rain storm, so I use two stalks and tie them together part-way up with a strip of rag or old sheeting, for stronger support, and retie them as the beans grow up.

Both sunflowers and pole beans need an all-season position, so I plant them at the lower end of my garden where they will not overshade any neighboring plants.

Sunflower stalks, with their rough texture, are more of an aid to the climbing beans than smooth surfaced poles or stakes, which have to be taken out of the garden and put somewhere, come fall, and four feet apart is not necessary. And using sunflowers for pole beans means no bending for the gardener as beans climb. And weeding at the base of the sunflowers is unnecessary once the beans start climbing.

Then I found it worked better to plant the sunflower seeds in a straight row. Sunflower seed has excellent germination and all I need to do is to thin the plants until I have two stalks close together. Not more than two feet apart. Just room enough to get around them and reach up for the pole beans as they climb the sunflowers.

When the sunflower plants have a head start of about two feet, I plant beans in a circle around them, six to eight inches away from their base, planting beans liberally. Once again it is easier to thin than transplant. I thin that circle of bean plants to the sturdiest four or five. Pole beans have heavy vines. As the sunflowers leaf out, I break or cut off the leaves just ahead of the bean vines as they reach for the knobby protuberances gratefully. If a bean vine is reluctant to twine up, it can be gently encouraged by turning the tendrils up and around the sunflower stalk. (In dry weather, not rainy weather.)

Keep ahead of the climbing bean vines by breaking or cutting off the huge sunflower leaves which would be in their way, and which would shut out sun and air. Also by moving the rags and strips of sheeting as the beans climb.

The green of the growing pole beans and the towering golden sunflower heads is quite spectacular. Beans for people and sunflower seed for birds.

Come deep frost, Hal would pull down the heavy sunflower stalks and cut off the flower heads for winter feeding for birds at their feeders. (If they hadn't done their own harvesting first.) And he would cut down the sunflower stalks, chop them up for the compost pile, or let them winter-rot in the garden ready for spring plowing.

To rotenone, it is quite easy to dust all through the climbing Kentucky Wonder or Italian flat-podded beans in a minute. The sunflowers don't need rotenone.

I have tried tomatoes up the sunflower plants but found they were too heavy even for the double stalks.

For freezing, mature beans are better than the young beans. But if you want to be lazy, all the climbing beans can be left on the sunflower stalks until brown and dried up. Then shelled, and boiled up for a vegetable or used in any recipe such as minestrone. Or boiled in the southern fashion with bacon or salt pork, or a ham bone for New England baked beans.

BEETS

Beet seed has the peculiar habit of being a multiple seed, each seed breaking up and forming a cluster of three or four plants. Germination is often poor. So if you space your seeds at intervals in the row you end up with too many seedlings in one spot and bare spots in the row. I got around this by planting the beet seeds very thick in a shallow furrow about three inches wide, strewing them down the center line and then pushing some to each side to make a wider row, then covering them and tamping them down. In this way I get young beet greens in my first thinning, then tender baby beets, and then mature beets. If I have planted seed thick enough there is practically no weeding necessary, the young seedlings lend support to each other instead of needing propping up after a rain, and we eat as I thin. Another thing I've found that is interesting is that the mature beets can be halfway out of the soil, looking almost like Siamese twins, and yet be perfect for eating. Their tops do not discolor or turn bitter, and as any cook knows, any blackish top can just be cut off after boiling the beets.

Most varieties of beets are now coreless and without those white rings throughout, and without woody fiber. Clear, clean red. One thing I advise against is trying so-called white beets. I tried them. They look like turnips and tasted mushy. I'll stand by any variety of red beet.

Young beet greens are a delicacy, as anyone who has bought them in the market, greenhouse grown, knows. And expensive. With my young beet thinnings, I rinse them in lukewarm water, boil them quickly, then chop in a colander. When beets are to be boiled, scrub them first and be sure to leave on almost two inches of their stems so that the beets will not bleed. But beets of all sizes can be peeled and sliced, cooked in a little butter and a small amount of boiling water till the liquid absorbs into the beets (watch the pan!), then served. About 10 minutes cooking time, and none of that heat in the kitchen, on a hot summer day.

Mature beets after boiling can be skinned easily by plunging them into cold water and slipping off the skins. Then cut into chunks for Harvard beets or sliced for a salad.

THE CABBAGE FAMILY

One of the most exciting and successful experiments in my whole garden is my transplant cabbage bed.

I stake out an oblong plot, about five feet long and no more than four feet wide, so I can get around it easily, and not sacrifice too much space for the seedling bed. (Later, space will be needed.) I plant seed of the whole cabbage family—early and late white cabbage, crinkly green Savoy cabbage, red cabbage, Brussels sprouts, broccoli and cauliflower—in this seedbed. I use the handle of a rake or hoe to mark shallow furrows for my guide lines. In the seedbed it is necessary to have markers because when the cabbage family puts up seedlings they all look alike, and I have found myself giving away cauliflower plants to someone who likes cabbage and doesn't like cauliflower, or Brussels sprouts to someone who hates Brussels sprouts, and finding myself with not enough Brussels sprouts, which I especially enjoy.

The advantage of the cabbage seedbed is that rotenoning can be done right across the whole small seedbed in a minute, to discourage flea beetles which might attack the young plants, or those pretty white butterflies which hover around to lay their eggs which turn into those green worms.

The seed germination is so prolific in all of the cabbage family that a four-fingered rake often has to be used to scratch through the seedbed, so that sufficient seedlings can mature to a transplant time.

Seeds can be planted just near ground level with only a tiny bit of soil coverage. No weeding is necessary. But I try to thin out some of that cabbage family in the plot to about two inches between plants. (And as the garden season progresses I leave some of the Brussels sprouts to mature right there.)

Cabbage, fresh from the garden, has a juiciness, tenderness and flavor that is never found in store-bought cabbage. I buy seed of early

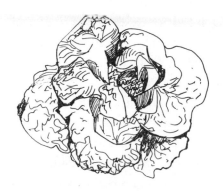

and late, round head or pointed cabbage. Any kind of crinkly green Savoy or red cabbage.

After transplanting, the heads of red cabbage among the other transplanted cabbages are magnificent. With their mamoth purple outside leaves and tightly curled solid red heads, they are beautiful enough to paint.

To transplant the cabbages, wait until the seedlings are about six to seven inches tall and all cut-worm damage is through. Select ones that have sturdy stems. Even if the stems are a little twisted, they will grow properly once they are transplanted. Dig your holes for transplanting first. Water the holes well if you have no rain to help you. And with cabbages—white, Savoy, or red—allow about two feet between plants. Those cabbages will have enormous leaves surrounding the solid cabbage head, and no weeding will be necessary. The leaves are worth putting on the compost heap as you pick the solid cabbage heads. But plan the space if you want cabbage.

Garden cabbage—white or green Savoy—is wonderful if it is shredded fine and cooked in boiling salted water for ten minutes. Or used for cole slaw. Or sauerkraut, if you wish. Or quartered for New England corned beef and cabbage. The crinkly green Savoy cooks faster, so it has to be watched.

Red cabbage presented a challenge. Shredded, it added color

to cole slaw. Or baked in a casserole with sweet and sour sauce. But this cook (me) was never pleased with the result.

I transplant all kinds of cabbages together—white, green, and red. But to transplant Brussels sprouts, broccoli or cauliflower, I put them in vegetable rows after I pull out the vegetables that have had their heavy yield. My way of natural rotation again. Dig the holes for the transplants, water them, put in the broccoli or Brussels sprouts or cauliflower seedlings, and forget weeding. They do not need as much space between plants as is necessary with regular cabbage.

Cauliflower, though I love it raw in florets for a raw vegetable platter, or boiled, has always been a chancey vegetable for me to grow. It too often has turned out grayish-speckled at the top, or undersized, or yellowish. Cauliflower needs its perfect whiteness for eye appeal. For serving cauliflower florets on a fresh vegetable platter, it is often necessary to scrape off the gray discolored tops. Cooking it with a slice of white bread will restore its whiteness. (But throw out the bread!) And the young leaves of green encircling the florets and part of the white stem are also tasty, when cooked, and have that same delicate cauliflower taste.

Broccoli, I now buy. It's nice to have it in your garden, and with no poisonous sprays, but it seems that in spite of all my rotenoning, and rinse after rinse in salted lukewarm water, I'm sure to

find some tiny green worms when I cook it. Some people just lift out
the floating green worms before serving or freezing, but I don't like
green worms. It's anybody's choice. Broccoli grows with a delicious
blue-green compact center head, and then when cut, smaller florets
appear at the sides. It is picked before yellow buds appear at the
flowering tops. The stalks are as delicious as the tops.

With broccoli—home-grown or bought—I strip the stalks, using
a sharp knife or a potato peeler at the bottom of the stems, pulling
it upward, to get rid of any possible tough coating fiber.

I always cut the broccoli into two-inch pieces, both stalks and
tops, for fast equal cooking time, to get its tenderest flavor. Hollandaise sauce or just butter, when hot; and French dressing or just
vinegar (vinaigrette) when served cold.

Unlike other cabbages, Brussels sprouts need a hard frost to
bring out their flavor. Those tiny little cabbage heads will keep on
growing all through fall on any sunny days. I have picked them in
cold that numbed my fingers, as late as Thanksgiving and Christmas. They grow nestled close to a long stem, and you pick from the
bottom of the stem, as they mature. Break them off with your fingers
or a knife, at the base of each sprout, plucking off the overhanging
leaves as you collect them. Your aim is to get hard-packed tight
blue-green sprouts.

Brussels sprouts are one of our choicest vegetables for eating or
freezing. I peel off the outer leaves, down to the hard tiny cabbage.

If they are purplish at the core, either from garden or supermarket, they are not prime. I cut them in half to find out, and throw any purplish ones out. And then quick boiling, in salted water, for less vitamin loss.

CARROTS

Carrots are a root crop. They grow down into the soil, not up above ground. The preparation for any root crop means loosening the soil below ground several inches. Then the soil is put back, seeds are planted at near ground level and covered. This trenching has to be done just before planting the seed so that the below-ground soil is still loose enough for the root crop to form. Otherwise you can end up with gnarled, twisted root vegetables.

I used to spend hours weeding and thinning carrots. Then I found a better way. Instead of planting a narrow row of carrots, I plant a wide row. I strew carrot seed very thickly right down the middle of the row, a width of three to four inches. Then I scatter those seeds to a width of about five inches with my sneakered feet, pushing loose dirt over the seeds and at the same time tamping down and firming the soil. If the carrot seed has been planted thick enough— carrot seed usually has excellent germination—I have virtually no problems of weeding or thinning and no need to go out after a rain to prop up fragile young carrot fronds. The thick planting across the row lends support to the carrots, and weeds don't get a chance to grow between the plants. Any late weeding can also be skipped, because by the time you have good-sized carrots they are maturing below ground level.

The thinning is equally simple. As the wide row of carrot fronds grows, a handful can be picked from time to time to see if baby carrots have formed. If they have, young raw carrots are delicious eating. If they are not yet ready, that handful goes on the compost heap. I keep thinning in this way, in different spots in the row, and end up with young carrots, then medium-sized carrots, then large carrots. Notice that no kneeling or back-bending is involved with this method—just casual thick strewing of seed, then equally casual thinning by the handful.

I try to put in short wide rows of carrots several times during the growing season just to be sure I won't run out of baby carrots. Seed can be planted early or late, with no worry about frost damage.

The more orange the carrot, the sweeter its flavor. If I pull out any carrots that are yellow at the core, or have any green showing, I throw them out. They won't be worth the cooking or the eating, and will have that carroty taste which people dislike. So do I. But an orange-colored carrot has a distinctive taste and flavor at any stage.

Baby raw carrots are a delicacy for a salad platter or hors d'oeuvre. Just scrub them with a brush, cut off their tops and leave their tails on, for easier finger eating. Medium-size carrots are wonderful cooked in chunks in boiling water, then drained and crisscrossed in the pan with a knife, then buttered, salted and peppered. Reheat, and serve. A different and unusual taste, even for people who think they don't like carrots. And the large carrots are so useful cut or diced, for soup and stews.

C O R N

Corn is probably the most prized of all garden vegetables, yet many gardeners consider it too difficult to attempt. It is easy to grow, but perhaps once again it is my method.

Instead of planting corn in hills (groups of seeds planted together) I strew corn generously in shallow furrows. (I find myself always chanting when I plant corn seed, "Two for me and one for the crows." Scarecrows don't work.) I thin the plants from time to time, first when they are about six inches tall and past the point of being nipped off by any birds, again when the stalks are about ten to twelve inches tall, then one more time if the stalks look too close together for growth. However, two or three cornstalks can be quite close together and still bear because the corn ears develop toward the top of the stalk so there is little interference toward maturity.

As well as planting closely in the rows I plant the rows close to each other, not more than two to two-and-a-half feet apart. At picking time I admit it's like going through a jungle, but with a bandanna around my head and in sleeved shirt and jeans, I get garden corn in a minimum of space.

And I don't weed corn! Instead, I hoe up dirt along the sides of the row against the stalks from time to time which chokes out weeds and adds support. Anyone who has ever gone out to a garden after

a driving wind or rainstorm knows the chore of straightening up
heavy stalks and shoveling dirt to anchor them again, as Hal and I
did. I avoid this both by hoeing-up dirt as the stalks grow sturdy and
my close-row planting.

Corn will grow in almost any soil. It needs little soil preparation, and thrives in dry, hot weather, days and nights. A severe
drought is sweet corn's best friend. The only caution is that you need
at least two rows back-to-back, no matter how short the rows, because
corn is wind pollinated and not bee pollinated. One row only, and
you'll have no filled-out kernels. (I did that once, too.)

I used to break off the suckers (the little side shoots off the main
stalk) until I found out that these suckers give added support.

Corn can be transplanted if the seedling still has the original
kernel attached to the root. Preferably after a rain. But those transplanted seedlings take as long to take hold—about ten days—as
planting new seed. So no gain to the gardener unless you want to
present some seedlings to someone who yearns for started corn.

Corn should be dusted with rotenone twice; once when the
seedlings are about ten inches high and have the center stalk forming, and again when the ears are in silk and the corn is tasseling.
This discourages ear worms and also smut (the grey mass that sometimes forms). Beyond the hoeing up occasionally, and twice rotenoning, that is all the tending that corn needs.

I've tried midget corn. It's interesting as a novelty but in the
same space you can grow regular corn with larger ears and a sweeter
flavor. Of all corn varieties, my choice is Butter and Sugar. I've tried
succession corn (several varieties at one planting) but too many times
I've had all the hybrid varieties come in at once with a burst of hot
weather. And therefore they are somewhat tasteless.

I've tried two kinds of cross-pollination. White corn planted in
your corn patch, with yellow corn nearby; and you get white corn
with some yellow kernels throughout the ears, adding sweetness and

flavor. And I've planted some Black Mexican (which has strange red and blue and black but very chewy kernels) near the regular yellow corn and ended up with tender, delicate corn with scattered colorful kernels.

Corn turns from sugar to starch so fast that to have water boiling as you pick and husk the ears is to get the corn at its sweetest. I've found that if you cook too many ears together, you'll lose some of that special sweetness, because the corn is overcooked. So I plan on separate pots for more than three or four ears, and I break them in half for faster cooking. Boil corn quickly, covered, no salt or sugar added, and when it smells corny, get it off the stove fast. If I'm not sure it's done, I test a kernel with a fork. Garden corn cooks fast, in five or six minutes and then continues to cook from its own heated cob. (Once we picked a dozen ears right from the garden for a friend, gave instructions on boiling water, and were later told that she had boiled it for an hour and it was still tough.)

If you have more ready corn than you have guests (or your own capacity) I've found that unhusked corn will keep in a closed brown paper bag in the refrigerator for a day. Almost as good as fresh. Certainly preferable to store-bought corn that "came in this morning" and turning fast to starchiness each hour, with no comparison to those succulent crunchy kernels of fresh garden-picked sweet corn.

HERBS

The growing of herbs can be an exotic and fascinating type of specialized gardening, whether grown in an English herb garden, or in a kitchen garden, or as a border for flower beds, or even pot-grown in the house. I have grown almost every type of herb right in my vegetable garden, but we prefer the natural flavor of fresh garden vegetables so I grow only a few herbs each year, the proven standbys, like sage and thyme for stuffing, oregano for flavoring in Italian cookery and soups, dill for fish or pickling, mint for iced drinks and mint-apple jelly, chives for Vichysoisse or minced fine with cream cheese or mixed with sour cream for baked potatoes, and of course the most welcome herb of all, parsley. I've given up on fennel with its lico-rice-tasting leaves and stalks, basil, summer savory, borage, chervil, rosemary, and so forth, and buy them dried and packed with the garden work done by experts.

Herbs grown from seed means meticulous weeding and thin-ning which seems senseless for herbs which I only use sparingly. Started plants from a nursery or greenhouse are inexpensive, and time-saving. Chives and mint spread rapidly so their position in your garden should be planned. Most gardeners will willingly give you clumps of chives, or mint roots from their established and prolific spreading beds.

I consider parsley a "must" for my garden. I grow parsley from seed in the garden where it will get full sun. I plant a few seeds in a short straight line, about three inches long, at the end of several rows, by the path. Parsley seeds take so long to germinate that I always soak them in warm water for a few days, before planting. Once parsley is established, I let some of it go to seed each year. The following year I plant fresh parsley seed about two inches from the parsley from the previous year, to be sure I have all the parsley I want. New parsley means weeding and thinning as the tiny feathery shoots come up, but well worth it to have strong sturdy plants with tall stems and sprigs ready to pluck. The parsley seedhead grows up from the middle of the plant on a thick hard stem, so if you don't want that plant to reseed, pick that stem, and the plant bears much longer.

The single American-type of parsley is supposed to be more choice to epicures than the moss type, but I think the moss type is easier to mince and the velvety sprigs more effective for garnish or for eating in hand.

In the fall, parsley roots can be cut to the ground and crown and roots repotted for indoor use, but the parsley is apt to be spindly with not too good a yield. In winter, fresh parsley seed planted in a pot of garden soil is easier to do and grows more luxuriantly.

If you grow herbs you will want to dry your own. For a while Hal and I picked bunches and tied them with strings and hung them in the attic. This made the attic wonderfully aromatic but it didn't especially help the flavor of the herbs. Then a friend told me how to dry herbs easily with all flavor held; cut your herbs, put the varieties in different bags, just brown grocery-store paper bags, tie them shut at the top, let the bags dangle from string at eye-level in any doorway in the house, and just reach out and tap the bag as you pass. It's a wonderful system. Looks somewhat eccentric to have brown paper bags hanging around to be tapped, but you can always explain it to any guests and let them play the game too.

In a few weeks, when the bags are opened, there are the dried tangy leaves and buds and stems in the bottom of the bags. I throw out the dried stems, and pack the herbs in labeled bottles. I use dark bottles with screw tops to keep out air and light, and the herbs keep for years, contrary to what you read about herbs. However, when I buy dried herbs, I find that I must throw some out from time to time because the flavor decreases. *Note:* no herbs should be stored in too warm a spot in the kitchen, even though it seems handier to have them by a stove and looks prettier.

Herbs are clean plants to grow, have practically no insect ene-mies. But twice we have had amusing experiences with animal invaders. Once we had a woodchuck who would amble in and eat cucumbers and then travel across the garden to eat dill. Cucumbers and dill, the only things he ate in the half-acre garden, evidently liking dill pickles even without vinegar. The other time was an experiment that failed: I bought expensive potted basil plants at a greenhouse and set them out all around the garden edges. I'd read that the odor of basil was obnoxious to woodchucks and rabbits and would keep them away from the garden. The basil flourished, it was no help at repelling woodchucks or rabbits, and worse, it attracted every cat for miles around. That finished me with basil, either grow-ing it or smelling it, for a while.

L E T T U C E   A N D   O T H E R   S A L A D   G R E E N S

You can grow your own salad greens year round, starting with first lettuce thinnings in early spring, then head lettuce all summer, endive and escarole through late fall, and witloof chicory (Belgian endive) throughout the winter. That sequence makes an interesting chal-lenge for a gardener to try once in a while, to have your own salad makings at hand at any time.

Hal and I filled a barrel with sand, put it in the root cellar, buried the crowns of the witloof chicory, watered it every other day to keep the sand moist, and the endive growing. Once was enough. My fingernails and hands got too much of a beating as I scrabbled through that sand for endive. From then on I bought endive. But I learned that endive, when store-bought, should be fat, short, and golden yellow. If the tips are green and the stalks spindly, it means that endive is not worth buying.

My method of growing head lettuce from transplanted seedlings is my greatest delight in the whole garden. The flavor of any fresh garden lettuce is unequaled. Far different from the spongy white lettuce that is often the only kind available in markets, often streaked with brown from heat, often cellophane wrapped.

I had never grown head lettuce and I always wanted to. Then I discovered the way to do it. Transplanting lettuce seedlings. I devote a whole strip of my garden to lettuce transplants, depending on how much lettuce I want. I stake out with sticks my first lettuce seedbed. I also stake out three or four more transplant beds. The beds should not be over two-and-a-half to three feet wide or they will be too hard to reach across. In my first seedbed I strew lettuce seed generously. Then, when the seedlings are three to four inches high, I pull out some lettuce seedlings for eating or salads, pulling them out by the roots for salads with tiny sliced radishes and thin-sliced scallions.

In the second staked-out plot I transplant the seedlings from the seedbed. Dig holes in the second bed (in a rain if possible) and put in the young seedlings, giving plenty of room in the second bed to aerate around those seedlings with a four-fingered tool, to loosen the soil if it gets caked, and allow room enough for each head lettuce to grow.

The first seedbed does not need marked rows. But all lettuces

look alike in their early stage. I continue the seedbed and transplant method ad infinitum through that whole strip. When that first seedbed is finished, I rake it smooth and plant lettuce seed again. Again depending on how much lettuce you want, and what varieties. I grow eight or nine varieties throughout the whole gardening season.

Caution—never plant radish seed in that first seedbed, as I did one year. Birds think radish seeds are made for them. And one year birds ripped my whole lettuce seedbed and scattered all the lettuce seed. Since then I plant five or six radish seeds in any vacant spot in the garden. About five seeds at a time, an inch apart, so that I always have crisp red radishes. I tamp and stamp on those five or six radish seeds, and found I could get ahead of the birds.

Germination of lettuce seed is always problematic. The most recent lettuce seed is what I usually plant first. Just to be sure. Then I follow up with the old seed. And often put lettuce seed in the freezer, hoping for better germination. Leftover seed is often better, with better germination.

That head lettuce is my pride and prize in the whole garden, looking as pretty as a bouquet. Each lettuce variety has its own distinctive flavor and texture, and although they can be mixed together for a garden tossed salad, it is absolute luxury to be able to use only one kind at a time and relish the differing tastes. Again it is a question of individual preference, whether the crisp iceberg type, the softer leaves of Salad Bowl, Boston, etc., the flat multicolored rosettes of the original southern bibb, the whole head with the root cut off served on a plate (I found that even with the most careful rinsing, there was too much sandy soil between its leaves); Oakleaf, which is so fragile and delicate that markets don't even carry it; Cos or romaine, tall with furled stalks that can be eaten in hand or used with a dip of Russian dressing or mayonnaise; and countless other varieties which are fun to try, to experiment with, to make your choices.

One year we had too much head lettuce all at the same time. I phoned some neighbors and friends. They had lettuce. Either their own, or given to them. After a few phone calls I decided I didn't have time to spend my day asking if people had lettuce! Hal and I decided to strip those beautiful ready lettuces down to their hearts. We both felt like vandals and I sort of looked around the corner to see if the state troopers were passing by as we shucked all outer leaves onto the compost heap. They didn't catch up with us.

Garden lettuce is usually used in a tossed salad. But I learned a new one. Wilted Lettuce, it is called in Colorado. First you cook bacon. Then remove the bacon from the pan, to add later. Then cut lettuce into short pieces, cook briefly in the bacon fat with a little chopped onion and sugar, and crumble the bacon into it, adding a little vinegar. It's good.

Endive and escarole will provide garden salad greens into late fall, past hard frost to Thanksgiving, sometimes till Christmas. I have even dug up heads in snowdrifts and found the blanched hearts still intact and tasty. Endive has tall curly leaves. Escarole is a wider-spreading plant with broad leaves. Both are grown in the same way and both form a yellowish buttery heart when trussed and blanched. Germination is usually terrific, so the criss-cross thinning with a long-handled fingered rake is often needed.

I plant them in late July or August, about two months before frost is expected, near my lettuce seedbed. When the seedling plants are three to four inches high, I transplant them in wet soil just as I do with lettuce, but with one pleasant difference. Instead of setting them into the lettuce plot, I put them in any nearby vacant spot that will be undisturbed for the rest of the growing season. I allow at least a foot between plants, and to save room I alternate the curly and the broadleaf plants.

When the green rosette of the escarole has grown a good heart, and when the curly leafed endive is filling out, they are trussed for

blanching. Paper-covered wire or strips of old sheeting can be used, or even cord. The purpose is to pull up together all the outside leaves of each plant securely enough to hold and protect the hearts, but loosely enough so that the plants can keep growing. This tie-up job is better done with four hands than two, one person holding the outside leaves in place, while the other puts on the tie. It is important that no lumps of soil or dead leaves or anything like that be caught up in the trussed leaves, or it will start a rot in the head. And it is wise to leave extra length on the tie for future loosening and trussing as the heads burgeon and need retying.

The trussing is rather a tedious job, but worth it later when you go out some frosty afternoon with most of the garden gone, pull a couple of heads, discard the sad-looking outer leaves, and find inside the delicious, clean, golden hearts, ready for a salad.

Instead of trying to weed around them and thinning, you can pull out both escarole and endive when the plants are young, cutting off the roots. Then cut them in small pieces and braise. (Sauté in hot butter in a fry pan.) Older leaves are too tough to braise.

Witloof chicory (also called French or Belgian endive) is the short, crisp, yellow, tightly curled stalks that you can find in the markets all winter. Or you can grow your own. It means planting in early spring, in all-summer position in the garden, roots dug up in

the fall and replanted in a cool place such as a root cellar or base-ment for new stalks to grow. For the garden procedure, deep trench-ing is necessary before planting to give depth for the roots, and extensive weeding and thinning is necessary to give sideways room for the plants of at least four to six inches apart. Plant seed at ground level and cover with soil. As germination is usually very thick, that means a lot of preparation and thinning and weeding for a busy gardener, so a short or half row is often preferable.

Just before hard frost in the fall, cut off the green leaves of the plants down to the crown, have a sandbox or barrel or large plastic container ready with sand or peat moss or sawdust, plant the crowns deep down, close together. Allow extra room above the crowns of at least eight inches. Unless the new blanched stalks grow com-pletely covered with whatever material you are using, the fat yellow heads that should be about four inches tall will be green-tipped. Watering is necessary from time to time to be sure of damp soil—not too wet and not too dry—or the crowns may rot or produce too-loose stalks. It's wonderful to be able to reach down into a barrel when snow is on the ground and lift out your own salad makings, but as a rule I'd rather let the professionals grow French endive and buy mine.

But I did discover that the deep-green leaves of the witloof chicory in the garden make one of the most effective backgrounds for a vegetable platter that I have ever found. So I usually plant three or four seeds about a foot apart and don't bother with trenching or weeding or sand boxes, just to have a few of those wide green leaves as a background for a raw vegetable plate.

In addition to these favorites of mine, there are the novelty salad greens, suggested by the seed catalogues every year. It is always a temptation to try them. I've found peppergrass (upland cress) and garden mustard worth a little garden space, but I grow them primarily for the tang they lend to a potato or vegetable salad when minced fine, or as a decorative sprig of green to garnish a finger-food plate. Both can be cut to the ground and will send up new tender leaves, so I only plant a few seeds in a small section of row, cover shallow with soil, then pick and cut off young plants.

Watercress gives an equally welcome tang, can be bought in markets, or grown by a brook, or picked wild beside a stream. And, of course, minced young dandelion leaves or minced young horseradish leaves can add pungency to a salad's flavor. Any of these are often used in a chef's salad or tossed salad by famous-for-food restaurants, but if you have a salad of your own greens—whether lettuce or escarole or Belgian endive—the most delicate of all dressings to bring out the individual flavor of each is just plain olive oil and vinegar and salt and pepper. With no additions or elaborate herb-blendings to complicate and disguise that fresh taste.

T H E   O N I O N   F A M I L Y

Onion plants can be bought at most seed houses, tiny plants with scarcely any bulb at all and with the green stems still attached. They must be planted when you get them, very carefully by hand, root-end down, at least two inches deep, and spaced three or four inches apart in the furrow, because they produce huge, mature onions. Some of my "plant" onions have grown to be five inches in diameter. One year I bought a hundred tiny plants—Spanish variety—did all the work of putting them in one by one, and ended up with several bushels of onions, far more than we could use. Meanwhile, they took up far too much growing space in my garden. So don't go all-out if you order some.

Any old sprouting onions you have in the house can be planted in the garden and will form new bulbs and shoots.

If I buy onion sets, I always buy white ones because I don't like to peel the yellow skin.

Onions do not winter-keep very well. They are apt to get soft and mushy or get black streaks through their layers.

An onion seedbed is a luxury I usually permit myself. I stake out an oblong about three feet long and about two feet wide, rake the soil very fine, strew onion seed lavishly (any white variety). Then I tamp down the soil firmly, all over the seedbed.

Quite a bit of weeding is required as the onion seeds shoot up, but after the seed has sprouted I pull only the weeds that will spread in diameter, like purslane, leaving any other weeds or grasses pur-posely. When the tiny white onion bulblets are large enough to eat, all I have to do is pluck a handful of weeds and I have a handful of tiny pearl onions. It looks terrible, that patch of weeds. But I know that that onion seedbed will give some of the most luxurious eating I know of; tiny onions boiled and buttered; tiny onions for the relish plate; tiny onions to pickle. I admit this is the most time-consuming thing I plant. That early weeding around tiny shoots. But sometimes a gardener enjoys just being in the sun, just sitting in one spot and weeding.

I also love garden-grown garlic. It's so much milder and more delicate in flavor than store-bought that there's no comparison. And young, green garlic tips are even milder. In fact, the shoots of new garlic are so wonderfully tender that I try to have a few plants growing in the garden all the time—just for the tips. I have bought garlic bulbs from seed stores, but I find that I can plant any old, tired bulbs I happen to have, or buy a package of garlic bulbs at the grocery store, and do equally well.

To plant garlic, just separate the cloves, stick them in the ground about two inches deep, and cover with dirt. They can be planted in early spring, all through summer, or in fall. I get best results with the cloves planted in the fall, and then wintered over, so I see to it that I have garlic planted in the fall.

I don't bother to weed or tend, but I always do have to stake out the spot in which I plant because the shoots look so much like blades of grass. The sure way to tell whether garlic or grass is to pick a piece and try it. No one can mistake the taste of garlic.

If we want to dig garlic bulbs after the tops have died down, we just dig up that spot with a spade, take out the bulbs and dry them. Hal even dug up garlic when snow was on the ground. A little garlic goes a long way.

Chives are perennials, and keep on growing every year once a few clumps are started. Those clumps spread from seed, from the beautiful lavender flower heads, almost as decorative as any known flower, but because they spread if not nipped off it is wise to plant chives on an edge of the garden proper, or as a border for a flower bed, or an herb garden, or just beside your house. They will grow in practically any soil, under almost any conditions, can be weeded or nonweeded.

Instead of the usual method of dividing and transplanting chive bulbs every few years, I use a simpler method. I spade up a few clumps every year, give them to somebody who wants them, or throw them on the compost heap. These cleared spots, neighboring the large plants, provide space and soil for reseeding and so we have young, blueish-green, tender chives at hand all season. And we know that with the first thaw of spring we shall have green chive tips thrusting through the tangle of chive brush for eating.

Quite often you can buy chive plants in the market. But I prefer those very strong-flavored shoots from the garden, particularly mixed with cream cheese for a sandwich.

Shallots—or, as the French call them, échalotes—are used extensively and impressively in French cuisine. They can be bought to eat or to plant, form bulbs like garlic, and can be separated into their cloves and replanted for propagation. I've grown them, but see no special need for them. If I want a mild onion taste for seasoning, either chives or seed onions provide it, or leeks.

Shallots are very expensive in the market, but they go a long way because each bulb forms a complete circle of new shallots around the original one and about three to four inches from it. Shallots can be braided around a string and look very attractive, but they have a tendency to dry out. I have found they keep better in the refrigerator. Not too long.

Tree onions are a novelty to grow near your chives and garlic bed. The bulbs grow at the top of the small tree and drop to the ground when they are edible. They have a heavy brown skin and you need to hunt for them right after they have dropped from the plant. Skinning them is impossible, unless they are boiled to loosen the strong skin. I think all the others of the onion family are easier to handle.

PEAS

I got tired of collecting brush for bush peas every spring, then having to carry it out of the garden when the peas were finished. It seemed like unnecessary work to hunt up branches of approximate size, pull off extra twigs, then push the ends of the branches securely into the soil. If a branch toppled over in the wind it meant damage to the pea vines and to the delicate tendrils which clung to the brush for support, and resetting brush disturbed the roots. Also, at picking time, I found myself jabbing my hands or knees on pointed or rough twigs, and missing pods which had been lost in the brush. Pea roots are very fragile and need support of some kind, so I tried using weeds for support and it worked.

Instead of trenching deep for a narrow row of peas, I plant shallow in two wide rows about two feet apart. I take a hoe, pull the surface soil to each side of the rows, a depth of about two inches, each row five to six inches wide. Then I strew the seed very thickly. (In one row I plant Little Marvel peas; in the other row, Blue Bantam.) It doesn't matter if the seeds come up close together. The thing that does matter is to plant plenty of seed so there will be no chance of bare spots in the row. I then pull that loose side dirt back over the seed and tamp down the ground very firmly.

To tend, I weed around the young vines only until they put out their first curly tendrils. Then I quit weeding. As the weeds grow

they give support to the vines, and add moisture and shade even in heat or drought.

With this system, I find I can plant peas much later then I ever dreamed of, as late as May first or May fifteenth, knowing I can count on those weeds against summer heat.

My choice is always Little Marvels and Blue Bantams. Little Marvel is early, with small tightly-packed pods, and has a tremendous yield. Blue Bantam is about ten days later, with deep bluish-green large pods, with an amazingly sweet flavor. I plant both kinds at the same time.

Peas are sometimes attacked by aphids, those small flying green insects. But a dusting of rotenone will take care of that.

I notice that after the first picking of the vines, that first yield, the vines tend to weaken and yellow and wither. So a second picking is all I can count on. Then I pull out the vines, strip them of pods, whatever the size, and regardless of blossoms. Even the tiny unformed peas give a special sweetness in the cooking.

Any variety of fresh-from-the-garden peas is unbelievable, and I can't resist testing and tasting when I go out to the garden to see if they are ready. (I can't even shell peas without eating some of them raw.) But if you are watching for the size of the peas in the pod, they can be estimated if the sun is back of the pod, or if the pea pods give a slight rattle as you brush over the vines with your fingers.

When the first yield of peas comes, I do my usual quick method with any fresh green vegetable—boiling water in a pan (no salt for peas, if you want their flavor) cover the pan, and by the time you take the lid off the peas should smell like the garden. One of the greatest delicacies any gardener knows. From time to time we would invite special guests to enjoy them with us. No matter what the rest of the planned lunch or dinner, the feast of peas was tops. How we all ate garden-fresh peas!

Leftover garden peas can be used with shrimp, or tuna, or for a salad. We never had any left over.

N E W   Z E A L A N D   S P I N A C H

New Zealand spinach is a "must" in my garden list. It can be used raw in a tossed salad and has enough body and flavor to enhance the salad. We particularly like it boiled as a pot green.

To plant it, I again go contrary to the packet directions. I plant two or three seeds together at ground level and another two or three seeds about a foot and a half beyond. These two hills of New Zealand spinach will provide enough for salads or boiling.

The seeds are somewhat large and tough. So if the outside covering is notched with a knife it will hasten the growth.

The plants are bug-free, weeds can grow all around the plants, and it is the cleanest spinach I have ever grown. The only trouble with it is that two-inch tips have to be cut off regularly, at least every other day. Each time a tip is cut off, two new tips develop. If the two-inch tips are not used immediately (you cook the whole tip) their stems will turn brownish and tired looking. Of all the novelty spinach varieties I have tried, it is the most satisfactory.

T H E   S Q U A S H   F A M I L Y

Squash, cucumber, melons, and pumpkins are similar enough to be grouped as a family, although the method of planting and harvesting may be very different.

Of course I have no trouble with winter squash, melons, and pumpkins, because I send their vines traveling over the weedy edges of my garden. But I must remember to turn their vines in the rain so they will not encroach on the rest of my garden. Once I had cucumbers trailing all over my tomatoes. A fine salad, but not in the garden.

The cucurbits, as they are called, have two types of blossoms, male and female. The male blossoms come first, on straight stems. Then the female blossoms appear, bulging slightly like a pregnant woman. The bulges will form the fruits. (This biological information seems to be unknown to many gardeners.)

In picking any squash, cucumbers, melons, or pumpkin (as well as tomatoes, peppers, and eggplant) it is wise to leave a quarter to half an inch of stem attached, and they will keep better.

I plant summer squash of three kinds—yellow, green, and white. I always get yellow squash seeds that are crookneck because they seem to have top flavor compared to the hybridized. For zucchini, I get seeds of the slim Italian marrow and of the usual green and of the mammoth black zucchini. The white summer squash is scalloped or patty pan. If you have ever seen the scalloped white in the supermarket, six or eight inches wide, which is watery, mushy, and tasteless, you will find it has no relation to the tiny patty pans you can grow in your garden. I pick the patty pans when they are less than three inches big, often with the blossom still on. Patty pan is delicious when cooked fast in boiling, salted water (with the lid on) and served with butter. Or sliced raw and eaten as a finger delicacy on a raw vegetable plate, using a dip, mayonnaise, or just salt and pepper.

I pick all summer squash—yellow, white, or green—when they are young and at their top flavor.

Summer squash needs plenty of space. One year I had a most amazing combination of taste and looks when they all crossed! One for the books, but not for me. So from then on I put pepper plants between them, or planted them in different sections of the garden. To plant summer squash, I plant in a two-foot circle, making a narrow furrow about two inches deep.

Because my Salisbury Garden is on one of the two major bird flyways, south to north, sharp-beaked birds enjoyed my squash seed. I got tired of replanting summer squash seed and asked Hal to do something about it. Cages or something. He did. He took chicken wire and made inverted baskets about two feet square and four inches deep. One for each circle of squash seed. By the time the squash plants reached the top of the chicken wire, bird damage was through and the baskets were stored away for the next summer. I then thinned the squash plants to about four to a circle, keeping the sturdiest.

Bush squash branches out, so four plants are all I dare leave in that circle. If one of those plants, well developed, begins to droop, its enemy is the root borer in the stem. Nothing to do then but to slit the stem of the squash plant and get rid of it. To avoid root borers I rotenone heavily around the roots and over the whole circle of squash and pile up dirt around each stem. My hoe-up system.

The leaves of the summer squash are prickly, so from time to time I cut off the lower leaves when picking summer squash. (Gloves are necessary, particularly if I have on a sleeveless dress.) In fact, summer squash plants are so prickly that I gave up planting them in any row and learned to plant them in circles, for less damage to me.

Winter squash includes the big Hubbards, blue, green, grey, or orange; the acorns; the butternuts; buttercups. And also really includes pumpkins. Winter squash is usually eaten after it is ripe, when the skin is hardened, after all-summer growth. Butternut is the only winter

squash that can be eaten at any stage of its growth, and is thin-skinned even when mature.

Of the winter squash we prefer buttercup, butternut, or acorn. Hubbard squash has a fine flavor, but one Hubbard squash is big enough for an army, unless you plan it for pies or freezing. Buttercup, green or orange squash with a turban cap at the blossom end, has a sweet dry flesh and less stringy pulp than Hubbard or acorn. It is our favorite winter squash and the hardest one to find in markets. Butternut squash has the smoothest flesh, with its bulbous end and meaty neck, with a flavor almost like a sweet potato. Acorn squash, small and fluted and acorn shape, is a general favorite for individual servings or stuffing recipes. Come fall, all markets carry winter squash at very low prices, and the taste is no different from your garden squash, so if you have a small garden I don't advise giving all-summer space to winter squash.

Winter squash is at its finest flavor if cut in half, seeds left in, placed cut side down in a dry pan, no water, baked in the oven until skin is easily pierced with a fork, then seeds scooped out and then seasoned to taste. Cooked with the seeds left in, the texture is juicier and sweeter than with seeds removed first, and it's certainly the easiest way to cook winter squash. It is so sweet after the seeds are removed that it needs no honey, brown sugar, or anything you might devise. It has its own sweetness.

When it comes to cucumbers there are so many kinds, sizes and shapes that the decision is a matter of individual preference—yours or your family's. I know people who will have only long, large, smooth-skinned cucumbers. Others (including myself) think there is nothing to equal the warty, knobby, crisp small cukes, so crisp and sweet that you can wipe them on your sleeve and eat them skin-and-all as you pick. The small cucumbers are of the pickling variety, oversized gherkins really, picked to be eaten when they are no more then three to four inches long and before the seeds have really begun to take shape in them. The long green glossy type is more available in markets, and keeps better as market produce. But these cucumbers need paring, and often seem to me somewhat bland and tasteless. Keeping quality and size are the usual market criteria, as with all bought vegetables. I often compromise by growing both types.

Some people like big yellow ripe cucumbers for eating or pick-ling. I pick my cucumbers steadily, even if I throw some out, to avoid the old yellow ones, and this seems to keep the vines bearing longer. And I caution anyone who comes into my garden to avoid stepping on the tiny vine ends, which can be fatal to the cukes.

I plant cucumber seed in any vacant space in the garden, and thin to a couple of plants. So I'll always have a cucumber on hand.

Note: most any variety of cucumber will climb up if you want to plan your garden that way, and plan on a fence or wire for it to climb on.

I have mixed feelings about cantaloupe and watermelon in my garden. They look alluring in the seed catalogues, but they need such a long season to ripen and require so much space for a comparatively small yield that it usually makes more sense to buy these members of the squash family in the markets at their prime. (They can't take a late frost in the spring and early frost in the fall does them in.)

I have tried midget watermelons that were supposed to be short-season melons, and they proved disappointing. One kind, a midget red, had several vines and only about six melons came to maturity. They were not much bigger than croquet balls and were somewhat tasteless. At that point I considered watermelon an extravagance in my garden.

Cantaloupe, on the other hand, has been a great success every time I've decided to give it garden space. But my luck has been primarily because of choice seed that was given me, including one that I understand was smuggled in by a soldier from an island off France that's famous for its melons. We found that the French cantaloupe ripened in the refrigerator, so we could pick it before the danger of frost.

One melon vine can run as much as ten feet in length with a spread of four to five feet. You can't expect more than five or six melons on a vine to reach maturity, so for a decent return you should plan on at least four plants.

Cantaloupes are ready for picking and eating when the rind becomes ridged with brown, and the connecting tiny stem attached to the vine dries up.

Pumpkins are a rewarding garden vegetable. Everybody knows what to do with a pumpkin—make a jack-o-lantern! You can also use it for pies, or pare and boil it for a vegetable, or even make pumpkin soup. Many cooks prefer to buy canned pumpkin or to buy pumpkin pies, both of which, of course, are usually Hubbard squash. But I like the "real" thing.

Pumpkins are grown like winter squash, seeds planted and covered, the blossoms and fruits growing along the trailing vine. Little care is necessary except to figure where you want the vines to travel.

BOUGHTEN PLANTS

I prefer gardening outdoors, working directly with the soil, to starting vegetables indoors, or in a hot or cold frame or greenhouse. This is primarily a question of saving my own time and effort. Young plant seedlings need light and sun, thinning and watering, and are too apt to damp-off or grow lank and spindly stems, or be at the wrong stage for putting in the garden when the garden is ready. So I let nurseries or greenhouses do the preliminary work.

Any time after the end of May, Hal and I would wait for a drenching rain to go to a greenhouse and get what he called "bough-ten plants," knowing full well that we would have the chore of getting those plants in the soil on that same rainy day—digging the holes, readying strips of newspapers to wrap tightly around each plant from just above the root to ground level to avoid any cutworm damage, and firming the plants. The plants may look a bit droopy the next day but they usually straighten up by the following day.

All young plants attract tiny flea beetles that can sap the leaves and kill the plants, so rotenone dusting is advisable every few days until the flea-beetle plague lets up. Dust lightly, because the young plants are still hothouse frail.

TOMATOES

When I buy tomato plants I like to get at least a half dozen pot-grown plants for early fruit, and then, for the main crop, those grown in flats. The individually grown plants are stronger and farther along, even to buds and blossoms, and can be put in the soil without any possibility of disturbing roots. Those half-dozen plants cost a little more per plant but nothing compared to buying tomatoes by the pound when your taste buds are hankering for the first red-ripe garden tomatoes.

Tomatoes can be allowed to sprawl in all directions over the ground but that means plenty of garden space, which few gardeners have. Some method of staking up is usually necessary. I've tried stakes seven feet tall, setting them before we put in the tomato plants, trimming the vines to a single stem, tying the vines at intervals as they grew with pieces of old sheeting or paper-covered wire twists,

and the tomatoes we got were beautiful but the yield was cut by all
the vine trimming. And the stakes had to be taken out of the garden
later! I've tried growing the vines up giant sunflower stalks, but tomato
vines are heavy and apt to pull over those stalks. I kept trying to
find the easiest way, but everything I tried meant too much preliminary work, all-summer work, and then fall work.

So Hal made A-frames that can be set up in the spring, folded
down and stored for the winter, brought out again and set up the
next spring. These trellises are made of 1" by 2" pine strips, six feet
tall and ten feet long. There are four uprights and four strips put on
lengthwise, the bottom one a foot and a half from the ground. Two
of these trellises are hinged together at the top to make one A-
frame. Or two, or three, or four, depending on how many tomatoes
you want, for yourself, your family, your guests, or for freezing or
canning. Set up in the garden, the legs spread about four feet apart
like a capital A, all is ready for planting the tomato plants along
each outer side.

As the vines grew, I tied them loosely to the long slats, and
they climbed and leaned on the trellises. The fruit was off the ground
and easy to pick. For weeds that grew under the frames, I spread a
strip of black building paper, sometimes called tar paper, but black
plastic could be used. The point is to have your only weeding necessary around the plants themselves, and then when the season is
over, just fold up the frames and store them for the winter. Any

carpenter or handy man could make these permanent frames.

As to elaborate pruning of the vines, I'm not in favor of it. Come a drought, or a combination of rain followed by hot weather and repeated often enough, all tomato vines are subject to blight. Browning of the leaves, tinges of hard whitish spots on the toma- toes, or cracking (store-bought as well as garden-grown) and if you take off too many vine leaves, the plant is more vulnerable to cli- mate and weather, and thus deprived of its leaf capacity for shade and continually ripening fruit.

Tomatoes ripen equally in shade or sun.

I like all shapes, sizes, colors and varieties of tomatoes, early to late, red to yellow. (Yellow tomatoes are supposed to be less acid.)

Miniature tomatoes are fun to grow, and wonderful to serve for hors d'oeuvres. As well as the usual red cherry, which has a tough skin, I like to grow other dwarf types which are thin-skinned, such as yellow cherry, red plum, yellow plum, and yellow pear, making a very colorful combination of colors and shapes.

Red cherry can usually be bought at a greenhouse or nursery, but the more novel varieties such as pear and plum miniatures are hard to find except through catalogues. My miniature tomato garden is always planned and planted away from my main tomato crop because the dwarfs may reseed and become a nuisance. I let the miniatures sprawl, as they will, in their separate garden spot, where I can pick from their small jungle, and then they can cross or reseed as they want, in following years. And I never bother with extensive weed- ing—just pick and enjoy.

PEPPERS

Peppers have a special place in my heart. They don't have to be weeded, need practically no care, have few enemies. The plants always look so small and stunted when I first set them out, seem to grow slowly, and suddenly they have blossoms and peppers. The plants are surprisingly brittle and a wind- or rainstorm can break off branches as they bush out, toppling over a section of blossoms and fruit. So, instead of weeding, I hoe up dirt around the young stems for support, then I let weeds grow around the plant.

I set them in the ground when I set out tomato plants. Peppers cannot take frost—they are one of the first garden plants to blacken with frost, and finish. (A good checkpoint for the gardener with early or late frost.)

I like the "bull-nosed" sweet peppers because they can be used for any recipe and are particularly fine for stuffed peppers because they are flat at the bottom and will sit up properly in a pan.

All sweet green peppers will turn red it you let them stay on the vine long enough, but they turn faster in warm, dry weather. The combination of red and green is most colorful in recipes or for salad decoration. But watch out for hot-pepper plants, red or green, unless you grow them for chili or Tabasco purposes. A little of that fiery taste, fresh or dried, goes a long way, as I found out once when I bought hot-pepper plants.

EGGPLANT

Eggplant is so beautiful growing in the garden with its exotic purple blossoms and its shiny purple fruits that I often buy a few plants in

spring. But too often, come fall, I have ended up with fruits between golfball and baseball size that must be picked before frost, just at the time when big, luscious, well-seeded eggplant is available in the markets at a very reasonable prices. I find little difference in garden or market flavor, and my plants have taken up space all summer.

The care of the plants is simple enough. Putting them in the ground, hoeing up dirt around the stems, then letting weeds grow for reinforcement around the mature stalk. And virtually no pest worries after first rotenone dust.

Eggplant, garden or bought, does not keep well, develops soft brownish spots unless used within a day or two. And it gets dark and of a mushy texture when frozen.

Batter-fried eggplant, or crisp broiled rounds, is a near-oyster yet definitely eggplant taste I crave each fall. And in casseroles, eggplant is superb.

Part 3

SPECIAL GARDENS

I am all in favor of That Weekend Place in the Country, with a small garden patch. Mind you, I said small. Who wants to spend precious days away from the city rat race trying to keep up with the rat race in a big garden? A big garden demands some time, labor, energy. There are ways around it, of course. My friends Sandra and Ricky worked out a system by inviting a crew of friends to their weekend place every week and set them to work, "good, healthful, outdoor work." They mowed the lawn, weeded the vegetable garden, and tended the flowers—and went back to the city exhausted. I often wondered how they managed to keep enough friends to have a fresh crew every weekend. Didn't they ever run out of friends?

But few weekenders have that kind of guile. Most of them have to do their own work, and after packing for the trip, getting food together, making the trip, opening the house, and unpacking, they run short of energy and enthusiasm for a garden. Especially when they think of reversing the whole process Sunday afternoon or bright and early Monday morning.

Therefore, the Weekend Garden should require a minimum of work and should include only easily grown vegetables which the family welcomes on the table. Yes, I know it is fun to show off, to go out to the garden and astonish guests with fat, ripe tomatoes fresh from the vine, the big, crisp bouquets of lettuce, and to say, "Come on, let's pick corn for dinner! The pot's on. We'll have the most delicious sweet corn you ever tasted." But it can't be done that easily. However, a good deal can be done with a little work.

A few basic items will make a very satisfactory Weekend Garden. Tomatoes, for instance. Six tomato plants set out as soon as danger of frost is past will pretty well take care of themselves and provide plenty of rich, red, ripe tomatoes by August. A lettuce seedbed will provide plants to be transplanted, and the transplants will make a whole succession of crisp, fresh heads for salad. Parsley seed planted as early as the soil can be worked will provide beautiful, tasty garnish all summer. A short row of onion sets put in the ground when the parsley is planted will give you scallions for salad for weeks to come. A few radish seeds planted every third or fourth week will give you sweet young radishes all season. A short row of bush beans, either green or wax, planted two or three times during the summer at three-week intervals will give a big yield of fresh beans. You can even grow cucumbers and have young cukes all summer if you plant a few seeds in May, a few more in June, and still more in July.

A short row of carrots and a short row of beets, planted early and repeated later if you like, will give you young carrots and baby beets for weeks on end. And they need virtually no weeding, cultivation, or preliminary thinning.

If you wish, you can put in mint, which will grow for years, and chives, which will spread and never die out. But those are somewhat beside the point. You can set out a couple or three pepper plants

when you set out your tomatoes, and they will give you fresh green peppers from early August till frost.

It ready depends primarily on what your friends and family like, and how ambitious you are. The vegetables I have mentioned do not demand much weeding or cultivation. Your garden will not be a show place, true; but it will produce. It will be even more generous with some attention, a minimum of cultivation, for instance, and maybe half an hour a weekend given to dusting with rotenone to discourage the insect pests. This job can even be skimped to an every-other-weekend schedule, if you don't get rain that washes off the rotenone a few hours after you put it on.

Some vegetables should be avoided in the Weekend Garden. Lima beans, for instance, need cultivation and early weeding, and they don't produce till late in the summer. Peas also take up room and must be picked when they are ready—let them wait a week and they are hard as bullets. Cabbage, broccoli, cauliflower, and Brussels sprouts have lots of insect enemies and they yield at the end of the summer, just when the weekender's summmer comes to an end. Parsnip isn't ready to eat till after frost. Besides, some of these vegetables are just about as good when bought in the market, so why spend your weekends coddling them?

Sweet corn takes up room, needs some attention, and really doesn't yield enough to make it worth-while for most weekenders. You can usually find a roadside stand somewhere in the area that sells perfectly good sweet corn. It won't be as good as garden corn, or as fresh, but it will be sweet corn that hasn't been two days on its way to market.

The important thing about a Weekend Garden is to keep it small and to grow only what you like. Don't waste time or energy growing vegetables that are almost as good when bought in the local markets. In fact, if I were a weekend gardener I would probably settle for a few tomato plants, a couple of pepper plants, a lettuce bed, a parsley bed, chives, and two or three part rows of bush beans. Those would take all the time I would want to give a garden. And even then I would think twice about some of them, remembering how long it takes to pick, wash, and prepare vegetables fresh from my own garden.

So make your choice, and check with the earlier chapters on those vegetables you choose. Keep the garden small. Plant part rows. Don't let a few weeds bully you. Make the garden work for you, not the other way round.

One amusing thing to try, for the weekend gardener, is to plant a couple of hills of old potatoes that have sprouted. Most people have old potatoes either in the city or in the country. Cut them in chunks and plant three or four chunks together, at least four inches deep, and each sprouting eye sends up vines. Plant a couple of hills about three feet apart.

Blossoms will appear at soil level, and when these blossoms turn brown it is time to dig young baby new potatoes.

The potato beetle is the one enemy of those two or three hills. So rotenoning should be done each weekend and soil mounded up around the plants because potatoes exposed to light turn greenish at the top.

THE SUMMER-AWAY GARDEN

It was Nancy who asked me how they could have a garden when they would be away all summer. She and Jerry were ardent gardeners. They were teachers, and this summer they wanted to go on a camping trip with their children.

"Just look at all this land," she said, "going to waste, when we both want to garden."

I looked. Their new house was on a flat hilltop and the grounds were in the usual state of a new house. Boards laid to get to the house, no lawn as yet, but all around the house was perhaps an acre of glacial drift, full of rocks. Not a shrub in sight. Just that bleak rocky sand.

"Oh, topsoil will be put on," she assured me. "And the boys at the school all want to help digging out the rocks. And I have millions of flower seeds ready. And herb seed. But can't we have any vegetables?"

They would be off late June after school closed, and return for school's opening in late September. I tried to think.

"And rabbits all over the place," she added.

Hmm, I thought. There were no fences of any kind, even as a mild deterrent. The cabbage family—broccoli, cauliflower, cabbages, and Brussels sprouts—was automatically out. And any succulent green-topped vegetables.

My list worked out this way. First, what vegetables they liked most, next, timing of planting to get the yield. The children adored raw carrots, and the whole family liked any and every kind of salad. So an early lettuce bed could go in and be transplanted to head lettuce for salads before they left. And early peas. Radishes and scallions, of course. Beet greens with young beets. Spinach, if they were brave enough to try it. (I've never had any luck with any spinach except New Zealand. And the bunnies would make short work of that once the house was deserted.) Early bush beans, wax and green, they would get.

Corn was out. Limas, with their tender green tips. Pole beans need rotenoning. Summer lettuce was out. Cucumbers and summer squash were out, without rotenone dusting.

But root crops are safe from marauders. If the tops are eaten off, the root still grows and send up more shoots as the root burgeons.

So beets, carrots, leeks, onion sets, parsnips, garlic, turnips, anything underground would be waiting for them in September. And all kinds of winter squash. Winter squashes often benefit if the tips of the vines are cropped off.

But the method of planting had to be different, for the root crops. Instead of thinning as they ate, the thinning had to be caluclated in the planting. Seeds at least three inches apart.

"Tomato plants I'd buy," I said. "And pepper plants. Nothing attacks pepper plants, and you may have tomatoes when you get back.

"If you like parsnips, dig some holes about eight inches deep and about two feet apart. Fill the holes with loose dirt and plant one seed per hole at ground level. Cover with loose soil. You might find wonderful parsnips, large and well-formed, when you get back, to dig in winter after frost. Parsnips need frost for a sweet flavor. They can be mashed, which is the usual way, but an even more delicious way of cooking parsnips is to cut them in rounds, about three-quarters of an inch thick, parboil, stick them in a broiler pan with salt, pepper and butter. A top parsnip recipe, even for people who always thought they dislike parsnips."

I looked out at that wide expanse of sand. "You can put in a few hills of potatoes, too. And in September you could plant a fall lettuce bed, curly chicory and broad-leaved endive. And tie them

up to blanch, for salads until December."

"What fun," Nancy said. "To come back to a garden."

I could just see those frustrated rabbits! But maybe they would make holiday on herbs and flowers.

The first week in June, Nancy wrote me a note, a good-by note, saying they were all set for their trip. And she added, "We have had green beans every day this week. And that's the end of the beans. The tomatoes are in and thriving. Peppers ditto. Carrots, beets, parsnips doing fine. And are the rabbits watching them! Winter squash has begun to travel, heading for the open spaces, looking for weeds to climb over. Potatoes are up a foot, and we have dusted them twice, but we haven't much hope—potato bugs come out of the woods, it seems. Anyway, the garden's in! And we are off."

They returned on schedule, the second week in September. I had a phone call the next day, not about the trip, but about the garden. It worked. They came home to find dead-ripe tomatoes, fat red sweet peppers, fine big carrots, enormous beets, leeks two inches in diameter, turnips bigger than baseballs, though they hadn't dug any. "And potatoes! Would you believe it? The vines were all chewed and withered, but I dug up three hills and got almost a peck of potatoes. They are small, but wonderfully firm and white inside."

Then she added, "I went out yesterday and planted a short row of endive seed. It probably won't have a chance, but it might, it just might, make plants to transplant. And if the weather holds we could even get a few heads to tie up and blanch."

The weather didn't hold. They didn't get their blanched endive. But practically everything else worked out.

So it can be done. It is possible to have a garden even if you are away from it practically all summer. A limited garden, of course, but still your own vegetables, your own produce.

THE CHILD'S GARDEN

The surest way to discourage children from gardening is to present them with a small plot of ground for neatly charted rows of carrots, beets, radishes, and so on. You may get away with the first seed planting and the first sprouts coming through . . . the "miracle of the seed" idea . . . but sooner or later the tending becomes a chore. "Have you practiced your scales?" Or, "Have you done your homework?" become alternates with "Have you weeded your garden?" And for what? To end up with carrots, beets, beans and radishes.

Why not let children plant things they like? Things worth watching and taking care of, like popcorn to be shelled and popped over a winter fire. Or peanuts—goobers, they are called in the South— with their yellowish-white flowered tops and the unbelievable excitement of pulling a plant and finding a whole cluster of real peanut shells clinging to the roots. Popcorn grows *up*, and peanuts grow *down*, so weeding can be skimped and the young gardener has popcorn for popping and raw peanuts for roasting. Any seed catalogue or packet gives directions.

Gourds of all shapes and colors are interesting and can be allowed to trail over weeds, out of the garden, like winter squash. Or a couple of pumpkin vines can trail off the side of the garden and, come Halloween, those tiny green balls have grown to orange, ready for jack-o-lanterns.

Any of the small-fruited tomatoes, red and yellow cherry, yellow plum and pear, are colorful to grow. They bear heavily, so only a few plants are needed.

To feel the thrill of ownership and accomplishment and achievement, the young gardener should have the pleasure of eating right from the garden. Tiny tomatoes, young tender radishes, or raw carrots. Radishes can get bitter or tough or maggoty. Garden dirt is a natural dirt and can be rubbed off on a shirt sleeve or a pantleg.

But it takes some garden experience to be equally nonchalant about beetles or bugs or worms. Carrots are good raw, but misshapen, gnarled roots can develop without thinning, differing too much from the smooth, regular, store-bought carrots.

Practically no care is needed to grow these crops. Naturally, any tools should fit the child's hands and height. A small rake, hoe, and one hand tool are enough. As to any possible bug care for young tomato plants, or peanuts or popcorn, pure rotenone dust can be put in a salt shaker and easily dusted on.

Four flowers, all easily grown from seed, which do not attract insect pests, are nasturtiums, Portulaca, Shirley poppies, and Petunias. They have varicolored blooms, but they are not usually picking flowers. They are better out of the vegetable garden. They prefer sandy soil. The minor investment in a packet of any of these, strewn at random in some vacant, sandy spot, should produce a prideful bouquet.

THE SIX-WEEKS-AWAY GARDEN

In a way, this special garden is based on the Summer-Away Garden. A couple of years after my teacher friends and I worked out the garden that would take care of itself while they were gone almost all summer, Hal and I agreed to go to Colorado for a five-week session of teaching in July and early August. And I thought, "There goes my garden for this year." Then I remembered the notes I had made, and the lists, with my teacher friends, and the way that garden had worked out.

We were better off, and so was our garden, than they had been, because we would be here till July. So I could grow the early crops. I got out my charts and records and made my own list. Then I planted accordingly.

Peas went in in early April. Lettuce was planted in the seedbed by mid-April. So were onion sets, radishes, beets, and carrots. I put in bush beans the third week in April, and covered them four times to save them from frost. They survived, and we had bush beans aplenty by the last week in June. The lettuce came along fast, and we had head lettuce, small heads but sweet and crisp, by mid-June. The beets provided the best baby beets and greens I have ever tasted. And we had those sweet, crisp baby carrots all through June.

Corn was out of the question, of course. So were the various cabbages, though I weakened at the last minute and bought late cabbage plants and set them out. That was a mistake. The rabbits, or something, didn't leave a trace of them. But late plantings of carrots, beets and parsnips, and onion sets, all put in the last week in June, did very well. I planted them very thin because they wouldn't even be up to thin or weed in the row before we left. And I planted winter squash.

And we put in two dozen tomato plants, a dozen pepper plants, extras so that we could lose half of them and still have a yield.

So July came, and we went west, leaving the garden to itself. It happened to be one of the hottest, driest summers in half a century, and long before we headed east again I had given up on the garden.

We got home the last week in August, and I was out in the garden before we had even opened our bags. I opened the gate, stared at the jungle of weeds, then walked out into it. And wanted to whoop with joy. That hot, dry summer had brought a bumper crop of ripe tomatoes, in large part because I wasn't here to pick them, impatient as always, before they were dead-ripe. It had reddened the peppers, dozens of big, sweet peppers. It had brought the winter squash to fruit early, apparently, for there were acorn, butternut, buttercup, and Hubbard ripening in the sun, out there in the deep weeds.

And down under leggy fronds of carrot top and slim, tall, red beet tops, trying to outreach the weeds, were fine, firm carrots and beets.

That was the year we canned 44 quarts of tomatoes. That was the year I had dozens of big, sweet red peppers stuffed with all manner of things in the freezer. That was the year I had more winter squash than I could give away.

I missed the corn, and I missed the midsummer lettuce. But I put out a lettuce seedbed that last week in August and we had head lettuce only a month later. I missed a good many of my usual garden crops, but we had enough to make us feel rich with garden bounty.

And I proved that you can go away for six weeks and still have a garden, early and late. All it takes is planning, calculating the time needed to bring a vegetable to readiness for the table, planting at the proper time, and knowing which ones will do with no care at all and still produce by the time you plan to get back. You will find growing charts, time to maturity, recommended planting dates, all the data you need in most seed catalogues. After that, it's up to you to see how ingenious you are, and how farsighted.

THE COLD-CLIMATE GARDEN

Who wants to grow a garden in Maine? Bobbie and Bill did. I was puzzled. They say, and it sometimes happens, "As Maine goes, so goes the nation." They also say that summer in Maine is one month: August. I thought of the rocky coast, the ice-chilling water I used to swim in, the rocky plateau of their property on a hilltop at Boothbay Harbor, and tried to figure out what Bobbie and Bill should do. They had about two months of vacationing time. No fence needed, no marauders—not even a bull moose. Perhaps a small layer of topsoil about two inches deep.

They could have a small salad garden with scallion tips, fastgrowing red radishes, and thinnings from Salad Bowl lettuce, or any loose-leaf lettuce that matures in around forty-five days. It worked.

If it were my summer place at Boothbay Harbor, I would also plan for the following year, by platting a small strip of land for all varieties of tiny tomatoes. Red cherry tomatoes, yellow pear and red pear, yellow plum and red plum, and let them reseed by themselves.

It's hard to find a catalogue with all these tiny tomatoes, but it would be fascinating to return the next year and find small tomatoes for an hors d'oeuvre plate or a salad. And after all, what else do you need with Maine lobsters from the lobster pots of a nearby village except a salad?

THE EASIEST GARDEN

The easiest garden in the world would be: Jerusalem artichokes, asparagus, rhubarb, chives, horse-radish, and mint. That is, if you don't want to spend any time taking care of the garden. The trouble is that all of these spread, except horse-radish, which you can have more of if you throw out some cuttings from the roots.

I cannot imagine what that garden would look like. In fact, I don't want to see that garden. With spreading plants everywhere, it might be the survival of the fittest. The Jerusalem artichoke or the rhubarb might take over the whole garden. Of course you could make a box stall for each of them, or put wire cages around them. Or generously give clumps of each away to friends (providing they bring their own spades and something to carry the shovels-for-plants and weeds and dirt). That would take care of thinning.

Once the roots are in the garden, they will grow by themselves, and you can skip all tending, spraying, and cultivation. They will take care of themselves for years. And you will have growing in that easy garden tubers of Jerusalem artichokes, spears of green asparagus, chives to be used in any recipe, sprigs of mint (whether spearmint, peppermint, the velvety-leafed Polish mint, or any other variety) for iced tea and mint juleps, and stalks of rhubarb for pies or sauce. The leaves of rhubarb are poisonous, but if you chop up some of the stalks and boil them in water, they will clean aluminum pans just as well as tomatoes do.

The preliminary steps for getting asparagus roots in the ground are quite simple. Decide how much asparagus you want, and set aside a plot for the roots. Once again, my method is contrary to the usual directions. Dig a trench at least three feet wide and at least a spadeful deep, pushing the top soil to each side. Then put in a layer at the bottom of that trench a couple of inches of dried manure. Pull some of the topsoil at the sides to cover the manure. Put in your asparagus roots, and pull the rest of the topsoil over them. You now have an asparagus bed. One-year roots to pick the next year is advised. I tried three-year roots and the next year had excellent large spears.

Asparagus was one of our favorite vegetables. We were almost

persuaded to buy a house once because the garden had about five-hundred thriving asparagus plants. But the kitchen was too tiny to cook in. A fortunate decision.

If you like asparagus enough to take a little time and trouble taking care of it, knowing it will last for at least twenty years, cut the ready spear at ground level, because it grows in a circle around that first luscious spear. Cutting below the surface will damage the surrounding spears. Tiny seedlings will crop up in all directions, but they are thin and tough. So let them grow, knowing that next year they will become well-bodied and well-formed. The asparagus bed, in fall, will be tall, feathery asparagus fern, the kind the florist sends with flowers. And bearing red berries. It is wise to have that feathery fern and berries cut down. And, come the first winter thaw, whether January or February, one spadeful from the asparagus bed will tell you whether or not the tips are coming through. If not, the whole asparagus bed can be spaded up, which will take care of quack grass that tries to outdo the asparagus.

To cook that garden-fresh asparagus, I found it was best to use a knife or a potato peeler up and down the stem to remove outer skin and the pointed scales along the stem that can harbor dirt after a heavy rain. My method of cooking it at that point is to break off the asparagus spear where it snaps easily, cut the stems in short pieces, and cook in boiling water with no salt. It is one of the tenderest vegetables there is, takes only a few minutes to cook. Seasoning can

always be added—butter, pepper and salt, or hollandaise sauce, but
it is usually so delightful right from the pan that we never took time
for hollandaise sauce.

Freezing asparagus never turned out well. Only the tips and
about three inches of the stalk held over properly. The commercially
packed, although expensive, is wiser. But I have used both tips and
the rest of the stalk for an essence of asparagus soup, to which I have
added milk and seasoning, for a quick cream soup.

A sauce of rhubarb, adding sugar to make it more palatable,
was considered by our great-grandmothers as a spring tonic, to "cleanse
the blood." If you like rhubarb, that is one way to handle it. We
never liked it that much. Tired blood? Fresh dandelion greens in a
salad or cooked in a pressure cooker seemed equally full of iron and
vitamins, come early spring.

Part 4

THE GARDEN COMES INTO THE KITCHEN

THE KEEPING AND
PRESERVING OF
VEGETABLES

*H*arvest time and the garden comes
into the kitchen. Not all at once, unfortunately, because you have
probably gone out and covered the tender vegetables like bush beans,
limas, summer squash, tomatoes, and pepper plants every time frost
threatened. Only to find the next day that no frost damage was
done, then uncover. It's almost a relief when frost really hits. By
then every vacant spot in the kitchen and the refrigerator is crammed
full of vegetables. But you have said good-by to most of that garden
till next year.

So what to do with all those vegetables? You don't want to
waste one bit of that garden that you have tended and encouraged
all season. And the vegetables are gleaming red and yellow and white
and green and orange and purple. And the kitchen is snug and warm.
No bugs to bother you, no rotenone spraying to be done, no part
row demanding your attention.

One rule I have always made for myself and kept to it. Each
garden vegetable has been wiped off with a wet paper towel the
minute it came into the house, then dried. I buy yards of white terry
cloth each year, cut it into yard lengths, then thoroughly dry all
vegetables, to be sure no blossom stains or soil will make them rot.
Any bath towel will do if you don't care how green or spotted it
becomes. I prefer the white terry cloth, because the whole batch of
toweling can be tossed in the washing machine together, then into
the dryer. It is just vegetable stains, after all. Nor do I care if the

terry cloth gets fringy. It can be used over and over again for the next vegetable drying.

It is a comfortable feeling to know that some of that harvest will be eaten right away and much of the excess can be frozen.

Some of the crops will be left in the garden for the sweetness that comes after a hard frost: parsnip, Brussels sprouts, and—if I have planted it—kale. Also out there are endive, broad-leafed escarole, as well as browned dried beans to be shelled, herbs, horse-radish, sunflowers, and perhaps a few flowers in the annual cutting bed that were brave enough to withstand hard frost. Tools yet to be put away, and the A-frames, if you used them that year—the end of the garden cleanup. But the garden is cold out there and you are warm and comfortable in the kitchen trying to figure out what to do with all the tender vegetables that you have lugged in.

I think I tried every method possible for holding vegetables for eating, or freezing. Carrots, of course, can be left in the ground till winter thaw. I have found that they are soggy. And if burried in sand they still lack the crispness that you expect from carrots. So my top method for holding turned out to be wrapping them singly in damp paper towels in the refrigerator and remoistening when necessary. Raw carrots freeze well. I wash them and pack them in plastic bags without blanching, freeze them just as they are. They come out garden-fresh, wonderful in casseroles or midwinter stews. I have also frozen carrots in slices or diced, handling them the same way, without blanching.

Beets can be kept anywhere, and cooked at any time. Summer squash and peppers get stuffed for the freezer. With any stuffing I can think up—rice, hamburg, chicken, corn, breadcrumbs, and so forth. But I do not cook the peppers first, whether red or green, so that the fresh garden taste is not lost when taken from the freezer to the oven. I have found that strips of red and green pepper to be used as a garnish or in a recipe turn slightly bitter when frozen.

Stuffing summer squash presents a different problem. I parboil the whole squash (in a pot of salted boiling water, perhaps five to ten minutes), then when it is cool enough to handle, cut it in half, scoop out the seeds and inner pulp to be mixed with your stuffing ingredients. I have found that lightly sautéed onions and cheese were especially good, topped with buttered crumbs. And they freeze very well with the outer skin left on and any mixture you want for the stuffing. All my friends say when I present them with stuffed squash, they know that cooking directions will "come with." Stuffed squash, stuffed peppers, or stuffed cucumbers seem to cook equally well frozen or thawed.

Sweet corn has always turned out best for me when cut off the cob and packaged for the freezer. Blanch the ears first, then cut off the corn kernels. Corn on the cob takes up too much room in the freezer, and the corncobs cook too long in the oven or in boiling water.

Raw onions can be peeled, chopped, and stored away in the freezer in Mason jars. Winter squash can be cooked and put into freezer containers. New Zealand spinach freezes very well if blanched, and packed tight in freezer containers. And tastes wonderful, come winter, served with a little vinegar or just butter. Beans, of all kinds, provide the biggest yield of any garden vegetable, and should be blanched for the freezer. Later, after frost, Brussels sprouts freeze well. (Also cauliflower and broccoli, if you want to freeze them. I have never had any luck with freezing red, green, or white cabbage.)

Tomatoes are the most difficult of all vegetables to keep or freeze. In the refrigerator, they turn soft. I have tried hanging the whole vine upside down in the basement. I don't advise it. Wrapping each tomato separately in newspaper and keeping them in a box seems the best way to hold them. I try to garner in before hard frost any tomatoes that have a tinge of color. I know these will ripen. But the newspaper wrapping means that they must be looked at often to be sure they are firm and have not gone rotten. Ripe tomatoes can be stewed up in a saucepan, and put in the freezer in Mason jars, ready to be added to any soup or recipe, or eaten as stewed tomatoes. Green tomatoes never seem to ripen properly. They can be used for pickling, if you want to pickle, or they can be frozen if sliced and sprinkled with cornmeal. To cook, fry in butter, adding brown sugar. The miniature tomatoes, even the cherry tomatoes with the tough skin, do not freeze well, although they look most picturesque topping a casserole of green zucchini.

Lettuce, I find, keeps best in a partially open plastic bag (so air can get to it) in the refrigerator. I do not wash it first. It is simple enough to rinse it off as you wish to use it, and if it is at all limp, it will freshen up if put in cold water with a little ice, then dried on paper towels. (Washing lettuce first and separating the leaves can too often result in brown streaks throughout the lettuce head.)

All cooked casseroles seem to keep surprisingly well in the freezer. Some, such as corn pudding, winter squash with apples, and yellow squash with onions, have in my experience kept for three or four years in the freezer, and tasted as delightful as when first cooked. To prepare casseroles, I prefer Pyrex dishes, aluminum foil over the top, and taped tightly all around, with contents and date marked on freezer tape, as well as what may have to be added when they are reheated.

As the cook will find out, salt loses potency in a frozen casserole

dish. But sugar does not. A wise cook once told me to add a pinch
of sugar to anything I cook, saying "It will enhance the flavor, but
you won't taste it."

Whether bought or your own, winter squash needs to be put in
a warm spot (I use a table beside the furnace) until "cured." This
means that butternut squash should turn a deep orange, and acorn,
buttercup and Hubbard should have a large orange spot on one side.
At which point all of these can be moved to a cooler place for stor-
age, or cooked.

Blanching is done only to stop the growing enzymes. There is
no danger of botulism or food poisoning in frozen vegetables, which
can develop in canned foods. I've tried some vegetables for the freezer
raw, and ended up with woody beans and rubbery summer squash.
Whereas the blanched vegetables keep the garden taste for a long
time.

My way of blanching is contrary to all freezing directions. I get
boiling water ready, cover with a lid so it will boil faster. I put the
ready vegetables in the boiling pot, watch carefully until the second
boil, then drain them immediately in a colander, either in a pan of
cold water with ice in it or under the cold-water faucet in the kitchen
sink. Then I dry them on terry cloth till they are cool enough to be
packaged for freezing.

This blanching process refers primarily to bush beans, New
Zealand spinach, Brussels sprouts (or cauliflower and broccoli if you
want to freeze them), and peas and limas if you have any left over.
We never did. Peas and limas and corn and asparagus are often better if packed commercially. Less work for the gardener. But with a
little bit of luck, the packaged commercial vegetables will not come
in a boil-in bag of butter sauce, but will be packaged according to
what your family needs are.

I'm a cook by guess and by golly, by testing and tasting. I make
no attempt to give exact proportions for any recipe. That is what

makes the cooking exciting. "Maybe this time I'll discover a new idea that will add a new flavor." Any cook is bound to vary a recipe slightly, depending on the timing or the preparation or the stove or microwave oven, or the altitude or ingredients on hand. How often in the middle of a recipe you find that exactly at that moment you seem to be out of something you thought you had in the house. I try to make it a firm cooking rule for myself that I set out all the ingredients necessary for any recipe I am planning to use. I learned that the hard way. Once I was attempting a recipe that called for garlic. I didn't have a garlic clove in the house. And my garden garlic had been all used up. I had no substitute for garlic except garlic salt, which I don't like, and which would have ruined that recipe. Another time I needed cream of mushroom soup. Of course, I had every other kind of soup that is made, but not cream of mushroom. Complete impasse. Until I got garlic for the one recipe and cream of mushroom soup for the other. Then I could proceed. Ever since then, I set out all and everything necessary before I begin.

I give myself (she said modestly) five stars for each recipe I include. But also ten demerits for every recipe I made that didn't suit me, and was then promptly thrown out. "Out," I would say to myself. "Avaunt! Scat! Begone!"

I find that if I'm cooking one casserole or recipe, it is just about as simple to make two. One to eat, and one for the freezer. Sometimes I triple or quadruple what I happen to be cooking at the moment. But when there were two writers in the house, I had to plan on immediate eating. (Writers get hungry, too.) When I do long-term simmering of spaghetti sauce or minestrone, I scribble notes in the kitchen on the current writing project.

I am starting with my own vegetable recipes that proved successful. And I am following up with a few special favorites. Please keep in mind that the ingredients are variable and my measurements are approximate.

HORS D'OEUVRES

RAW VEGETABLE PLATTER

My favorite hors d'oeuvre during the gardening season is a platter of raw garden-fresh baby vegetables. Baby carrots, whole, only two inches long; tiny seed onions smaller than your fingernail; young yellow squash, green zucchini and white patty pan sliced in thin strips; miniature tomatoes—red cherry tomatoes and yellow pear and yellow plum and yellow cherry tomatoes; baby cucumbers (the warty pickling kind) cut in quarter strips with the skins on; tiny crisp red radishes cut in rosettes; florets of white cauliflower. As any cook knows, the color appeal is always important. I prepare the garden vegetables ahead of time, put them in the refrigerator until they are well-chilled—separately, so the flavors will be individual.

As a background for the raw vegetable platter a couple of witloof chicory leaves provide a stunning background, with probably some kind of a small dip dish in the center—mayonnaise or whatever you wish. Often just salt and pepper keeps the flavors more distinct.

If I do not have any witloof chicory leaves, I strip head lettuce down to the hearts and put each tiny vegetable on a separate crisp lettuce leaf. (The hearts of lettuce are usually eaten up.)

DRY BEANS MARINADE

For a fall hors d'oeuvre I do Dry Beans Marinade. Any kind of dried beans that are still part green will do—Kentucky Wonders or limas are good. Shell them and put them in a marinade of oil and vinegar and plenty of crushed garlic cloves, adding any herbs you want. (Cover the dish tightly or your refrigerator will take up the odor.) Leave in the refrigerator overnight, and after draining serve with toothpicks and plenty of paper napkins.

PARSNIP CRISPS

Come winter, when the parsnips have had frost to bring out their sweetness and flavor, I do Parsnip Crisps. Scrape off some of the outer skin, parboil for about 7 minutes, then cut each parsnip into thin rounds, about half-an-inch thick. Butter them and place under the broiler. (I use a cookie sheet.) When they are golden brown, turn them once and serve them with a dip of sour cream and horse-radish. Even people who don't like parsnips like parsnip crisps.

VICHYSSOISE AND OTHER
ESSENCE-OF-VEGETABLE SOUPS

It's vichyssoise if you use leeks. It's potato soup if you use onions. The recipe turns out with the same approximate flavor, whatever

you call it, served hot or cold. I've collected so many recipes for authentic vichyssoise with all sorts of variations, including chicken broth and beaten egg and consommé, but I have thrown them all away. I make potato soup and call it vichyssoise, and nobody knows the difference. And onions give a better flavor.

You will need:

Potatoes
Onions
Pascal celery
Parsley and chives
Salt and pepper

Peel the potatoes, slice them into jagged chunks. (Jagged pieces of potato cook unevenly with over- and underdone ends, which is my aim.) I cut onions in chunks the same way. And pieces of outer stalks of pascal celery, with the fresh leaves. (This is all going to be put through a sieve or blender, so looks for once don't matter. The proportions can be varied, but measurements for the basic recipe would be twice the amount of potatoes to the celery and onion.

Put potatoes, onions (or leeks) and celery in boiling salted water. Bring to a quick boil. When vegetables are fork-tender but still crunchy, put through a sieve or blender. This is the essence of potato soup or vichyssoise, and it can be stored in Mason jars in the freezer.

Many other garden vegetables can be used like essence of

vichyssoise, with milk or cream added before serving. Cream of lettuce, cream of tips and ends of asparagus, cream of yellow summer squash, cream of corn, cream of New Zealand Spinach. These essences take up less room in your refrigerator or freezer.

To serve, I add milk, or cream, bring to under boiling point, add more salt and pepper if necessary, being sure that the texture is on the thickish side. Sprinkle with minced parsley or chives, add a bit of butter to each serving, and paprika.

BORSCH

It was a sweltering summer day. Too hot to garden, too dry to get fishing worms, too hot to do anything. Hal felt the same way. "I'm going to mow the lawn," he said. "I'm going to make soup," I said. And we both asked, "In this heat?"

Out there in my garden were burgeoning heads of cabbage, mature beets, carrots ready to use, and dead-ripe tomatoes. So I had all the makings for borsch.

There are many ways to spell borsch—borscht, borsch, borsht—and many ways to vary it. And paraphrase Kipling, "and every single one of them is right." You can make it with mashed potatoes, chunks of beef, hamburg, but for me, borsch has to have plenty of cabbage and beets. And if you have dead-ripe tomatoes, so much the better.

I looked through every cookbook I could find, but all the recipes for borsch differed. So I concocted my own borsch. I decided to start with about a cup each of chopped carrots, onions, beets, and sliced cabbage. I grabbed aluminum containers, big ones, dishpan size, made a quick trip to the garden, and picked. Came in. Started to chop. My cupfuls didn't come out even. Might as well double the recipe, I decided.

I went out to the garden again. Came back. Chopped. I had too many carrots. Not enough onions. I began measuring one cup each of carrots, onions, beets into separate pans. Ran out to the garden again. Back. Chopped. Sliced. By now the stock I had been boiling for the vegetables and the jars sterilizing in an open pan were making the kitchen somewhat hot. And I had too many beets, too much cabbage. Oh, well, I like plenty of beets and cabbage in my borsch, I thought.

I combined in an aluminum pot. Too small. I combined in a larger pot. Started that, covered with boiling consommé. I went out to the garden again for the tomatoes. Skinned them, cut in chunks. I was up to four times as much as I had planned, now. I cooked it and cooked it, and nothing seemed done, so I kept on cooking it. Testing, tasting, and pretty tired of borsch.

And Hal came into the house. I'd just added another can of consommé. "What smells so good?" "Borsch," I said wearily. "It didn't work out right." He took one look at the kitchen, wiped the sweat off me with a towel he was swiping at himself with, and began to laugh. It was my first minute to look at the kitchen. Every pot and pan and bowl in the house cluttered every inch of counter space. I hadn't known I had so many pots and pans and bowls. He started in at the sink, cleaning up. He tried the borsch, ate three bowlfuls. "Wonderful!" I couldn't even taste it. He put it in the mason jars, sealed them. And the next day, when I could taste, I found it was one of the best soups I ever made.

Since then, I usually double or triple it. But for a single recipe, you will need:

> *Beef stock or chicken stock, or 1 can consommé or bouillon (diluted with water, if condensed), or bouillon cubes dissolved in boiling water*
>
> *1 Cup chopped raw carrot*
>
> *1 Cup chopped raw onion*

2 Tablespoons butter or chicken fat
4 Cups tomatoes, peeled and chopped
2 Cups chopped beets
1½ Cups shredded raw cabbage

Cook all the vegetables in the boiling stock, consommé, or bouillon. Add the butter or chicken fat later. Borsch is supposed to be sweet. Beets are sweet, carrots are sweet. So test and taste. More consommé or bouillon may be necessary. Pepper may be added, but rarely salt.

Borsch is often served with a dollop of sour cream.

I shall make borsch again next summer. Just as soon as the cabbage, carrots, onions, beets, and tomatoes are ready. I'll be ready too.

GARDEN MINESTRONE

There are times when you wish you had something cooked that will last for three or four days when you want to skip cooking and do something else. My answer is this hearty soup which I can cook ahead, freeze, put in Mason jars in the refrigerator, or just keep eating. I consider it my most delectable soup. So do others. It takes some time to make it, because of the timing, but the results are worth it. You can't miss. And there is that wonderful soup in Mason jars in the refrigerator or in the freezer to be defrosted.

When I make soup, I make soup—quarts of it for immediate eating and for the freezer. I start with garden vegetables brought into the kitchen. Then I try to figure out what I need most for that minestrone. You will need:

Beef stock and chicken stock (or canned consommé, chicken broth,
*   or bouillon cubes dissolved in boiling water)*
Lima beans or peas, if you have any
Chopped onions
Bush beans cut in bite-size pieces
Chopped cabbage
Chopped celery
Chopped carrots
Diced potatoes (hold in cold water)
Pasta of all kinds (hold)
1 Can kidney or pinto beans (hold)
1 Can chick peas (hold)
Any leftover spinach, chopped
Chopped lettuce, if you want to put it in
Any leftover scraps of beef, hamburger, chicken, or chopped chicken
*   giblets*
Garlic cloves cut in thirds
A lot of parsley
2 Tablespoons olive oil
Rosemary
Thyme
Salt and pepper to taste

Cook the raw vegetables, except the potatoes, in chicken and beef stock.

When the vegetables are somewhat tender, after about a half-hour, add the kidney beans and chick peas, with the juice from the cans, thyme, rosemary, any scraps of cooked beef, chicken or chicken gizzards, chopped. Salt and pepper to taste. Then add the pasta and when it is nearly done add the diced potatoes and parsley. Then add two tablespoons of olive oil. (Potatoes get too soggy if cooked with the vegetables, particularly if the soup is to be frozen, and the pasta and potatoes will absorb a great deal of the salt. This minestrone is going to be heated up again either from the refrigerator or the freezer, so the soup should not be overcooked.)

My aim is to have a green soup the first time around, hence I use quite a bit of parsley and any old lettuce or chopped lettuce and plenty of cut green beans. For future servings, if you tire of the green soup, skinned fresh tomatoes or stewed tomatoes or grated cheese can be added. But never skip the olive oil or rosemary. They are the ingredients that give that special flavor.

A tossed green salad is the perfect accompaniment for this hearty soup.

SALADS

TEN-MINUTE POTATO SALAD

With potatoes in the garden and hard-boiled eggs in the house, I'm ready all summer long for an unexpected guest or two. This potato salad takes me only ten minutes, but I was somewhat surprised when it took a helpful teenager two hours to make it under my direction! You will need:

> *Potatoes*
> *Hard-boiled eggs*
> *Red radishes*
> *Parsley*
> *Dry mustard*
> *Vinegar*
> *Salt, pepper, and paprika*

Peel potatoes and slice in half-inch slices. Cook in boiling salted water for five minutes. Drain, place in shallow bowl. Add dry mustard and chopped-up boiled egg. Add some vinegar. Hold the parsley (because vinegar will change its color). Add at the last minute. Add tiny slivered red radishes for tang. (A bit of wild mustard or a bit of snipped dandelion stems or a snipped horse-radish leaf, if you have them. Famous New York City restaurateurs use mustard cress for tang, I understand. So why not me?)

I add no mayonnaise at this point. Perhaps I shall on the next day if I have any left over, but I seldom do. (I often make enough potato salad to add either cooked bush beans or cooked beets, either of which provide extended use of that potato salad.)

And, with the delightful salad in the kitchen, I am happily out in the garden.

SORE-THROAT ASPIC

I am always sorry when the garden tomatoes are finished. "There go my bacon, lettuce, and tomato sandwiches," I think. But I find that a few days later my desolation at the wonderful garden tomatoes leaves me. I begin to think of how good Sore-Throat Aspic is going to taste. The reason I call this "Sore-Throat Aspic" is that everybody I know is so delighted to have it at a time when they don't want to eat anything because of a cold or sore throat.

During the peak of the lemon crop in the markets I buy and juice lemons, and keep the juice in plastic ice-cube trays in the freezer. And I usually have a box of unflavored gelatin handy. Simply enough to make my own lemon gelatin, but I often settle for a package of lemon Jello.

You will need:

½ *Cup water*

1 *Regular-size box of lemon gelatin*

1¾ *Cups of thick garden-tomato juice*

1 *Tablespoon vinegar*

1 *Pinch of salt*

Chives or onions, and parsley

Boil up some water. Use one-half cup to dissolve the gelatin. (I use a Pyrex pitcher for easier pouring.) Then add the rest of the liquid. Add one tablespoon of vinegar and a pinch of salt. (Sore throats don't take too kindly to too much vinegar, salt, or pepper.) Pour the aspic in small Pyrex cups.

Then with the kitchen scissors I cut a little minced parsley for pretty, and some tiny bits of chives if I'm lucky enough to have them. (If I do not have chives I use a bit of finely minced onion, but not too much.) I sprinkle these over each cup of aspic, cover with plastic wrap and chill in the refrigerator. The aspic will toughen without the plastic wrap, unless it is eaten as soon as firm.

VEGETABLE CASSEROLES

GARDEN YELLOW SUMMER SQUASH CASSEROLE

I've only known two people who were really stubborn about yellow squash. One was Maudie, a tart little old lady who would eat everything else I cooked. It became a joke with her about this casserole. "Summer squash? I wouldn't eat the stuff," she said firmly for years. Finally I gave her a casserole from the refrigerator to take home.

Two nights later she phoned me, "Give me that recipe at once. I ate it for lunch and dinner for two days and wanted twice as much." Then she added, "and whenever I can get squash I'm going to make it myself."

The other sale was by chance. Diana had warned me that Jim wouldn't eat squash, but would I cook some for her. I had all sorts of other garden vegetables with the meal, but Jim kept asking for seconds then thirds of the squash-and-onion casserole. "Get that recipe," he told his bride.

It's such an easy recipe. The only difficulty is to be sure you have enough summer squash, because all squash cooks down. It is disconcerting to plan two or four casseroles and end up with only one or two.

Get buttered casseroles ready and waiting. You will need:

Large summer squash
White onions
Cream
Butter
Buttered bread crumbs
Salt and pepper

Slice the unpeeled squash in rings about one-half inch thick. Slice the white onions quite thin. Then cook the squash rings and onion rings in boiling salted water for about ten minutes. Drain, place in the casserole, add at least half a cup of cream, extra butter and salt and pepper. Then taste. All squash is insipid unless it has plenty of butter and salt and pepper, and the cream will nullify some of the onion and squash taste. Top with buttered bread crumbs, bake in a 375° oven until crumbs are golden brown.

This is for the casserole you plan to eat immediately. For extra casseroles for the freezer or refrigerator, the casseroles should be covered when baked to allow for later browning of the bread crumbs. An aluminum foil cover is sufficient for the refrigerator or the freezer. But on the second warming up you will find that a great deal of the cream has been absorbed. So I always add extra cream or milk, using a knife to make room on the sides of the casseroles. Lower your oven temperature to 300° or 275° till the casserole has heated through to the bubbly point and crumbs are brown.

Onion is a pervasive taste, so the proportion of squash to onion is about three to one. And this is one of the few vegetable casseroles that I make for which I prefer a fairly good-size squash, rather than the tinies. More flavor. Too-old squash have too-tough skins. But you can test with your fingernail, which should pierce the outer skin immediately, and show whether the outer skin is tender enough. This is easy to do with your own garden squashes, although I wonder what the markets might say if all their summer squash were finger-nailed.

GARDEN WINTER SQUASH AND APPLE CASSEROLE

This is very easy to make for immediate eating or for freezing. Everybody I've served it to exclaims over it, and it's so easy to make that I always try to have it at hand either from my own butternut squash or store-bought in the fall when both squash and apples are available and inexpensive. I think it is best with roast pork or ham, but come Thanksgiving and turkey time I know that when I ask Margaret "What can I bring?" she will always answer, "Oh, have you one of those yummy butternut casseroles?"

You will need:

Any kind of apples
Butternut squash
Brown sugar
Butter or margarine
Salt and pepper
Paprika

(Butternut squash with its smooth, firm, orange-colored flesh is the only winter squash I make this with. There is no pith or fiber.)

Have your buttered casseroles waiting with covers ready.

Cut the butternut squashes into rounds about half-an-inch thick. Peel off the rind generously, so that no greenish or whitish edges are left. Scoop out all seeds and pulp. Core the apples, peel them and slice into half-inch rounds. You will now have rounds of cored apple and butternut squash. The most perfect rounds will go on the top of the casserole. The meaty neck slices of the squash and any apple rings you broke are for the bottom layers.

Make layers of apple and squash, adding butter, brown sugar, salt and pepper as you go. There are no measurements that can be given for this, but like all squash and raw apple dishes, this will cook down, so I plan on proportions of ⅔ squash and ⅓ apple. It is delicious any way you do it.

Sprinkle a little paprika on the top rings for pretty.

Your aim is to have the brown-sugar sauce and butter candy the squash and apples, but not to let the brown sugar burn on the bottom. I cook this casserole covered for a half hour at 250°, then turn up the heat to around 300° for an hour.

For freezing, I use the same method as for the preliminary cooking (one half-hour in a slow oven). Then the partially-cooked casserole goes into the freezer with an aluminum-foil cover.

Note: I have never yet made these casseroles without finding that they cook down to about one-half their original volume, so you

may have to combine more squash and apples to get them suffi-
ciently filled, and replace the pretty open rounds on the tops. The
top must look inviting. The taste, I know, is there.

GARDEN EGGPLANT CASSEROLE

Come fall I begin to hanker for this casserole, so if I haven't grown
eggplant in my garden I buy it. And I find that people who wouldn't
touch eggplant battered and fried or stuffed also like it. Sara and
Charles thought it was the easiest and most delicious way of using
eggplant that they had ever known.

You will need:

Eggplants
Pascal celery
Bread crumbs
Butter
Salt and pepper

Pare the eggplant past any possible greenish rind, dice, cook in
salted boiling water for 10 to 15 minutes until tender but not mushy.
The eggplant is going to be baked later. Drain the eggplant, place
in buttered casserole, add minced raw celery, plenty of butter, salt
and pepper, top with the buttered crumbs, bake about half an hour
at 350° until the crumbs are golden brown.

The texture of the raw celery combined with the soft eggplant
is what makes this recipe. There is no hint of the sometimes bitter
taste of eggplant. Keep in mind that eggplant will cook down most
deceptively. A very extravagant way with eggplant compared to frying
it, but well worth it when eggplant is in season.

LIMA BEAN AND RED CABBAGE CASSEROLE

I always have the problem of what to do with red cabbage. I grow it mainly because it looks so magnificent in the garden, with its beautiful red and purple leaves spreading out like a painting. But after light frost, when I have them stored in the refrigerator, there comes a time when cabbage is taking up too much space. So out come the cookbooks as I wrestle once more with caraway, sweet-and-sour sauces, grapes, onions, or whatever, knowing full well that I've never yet found a red cabbage casserole I like. So I concocted one.

You will need:

Red cabbage
Bacon and bacon fat
Shelled fat lima beans (large green limas)
Vinegar
Salt and pepper

The big fat meaty lima beans are the secret of this recipe—the green of the beans contrasted with the red cabbage for color, and the contrast of texture between the two vegetables.

Fry several slices of bacon till crisp, and crumble them on a piece of paper toweling. Save the bacon grease. Slice the red cabbage very thin, then cut it through with a knife, boil fast in salted water with a little vinegar added so that it won't lose its color. Place drained cooked cabbage, bacon, bacon fat, and lima beans in a Pyrex dish. Cook uncovered in a 375° oven for about an hour. (This recipe can also be made with canned butter beans.)

This casserole was an experiment that worked. I haven't frozen it yet. We haven't had enough left over to try.

GARDEN-STUFFED ZUCCHINI

I'm delighted to say that this stuffed zucchini will keep perfectly in the freezer, even for two or three years! It takes quite a bit of work and time if you are doing it for the freezer, but is worth it because it makes an unusual vegetable accompaniment for steak, roast beef, lamb, or broiled chicken, any time of the year. It can also be prepared for immediate eating, but I wouldn't put in the time necessary unless I were cooking for a large family or had a number of guests about to arrive.

You will need:

Zucchini squash
New Zealand spinach
Vegetable oil
Bread crumbs
Eggs
Onions
Garlic
Green peppers
Celery
Paprika
Salt and pepper

Proportions are problematical. It all depends on how many zucchinis you are stuffing—and whether for the freezer or for immediate use. All I can say is, have enough of all ingredients on hand.

Any kind or size of zucchini will do—cocozelle, or Italian marrow Caserta, or the blackish eggplant type—is still young enough to have a fingernail go into the skin for testing, and without overdeveloped seeds. For serving as a main vegetable on a plate with meat, half a young zucchini is prettier than a larger piece . . . but it is good either way.

First I see to it that the spinach is washed, cooked, and drained. Then put it aside. Next, I parboil the zucchini squashes for about ten minutes. I put them aside on a cookie sheet or in a roasting pan to let them cool enough to handle. While the spinach is draining and the zucchini are cooling, I mince celery, parsley, and green peppers, chop onions, and get bread crumbs ready in a plate or pan. (By this time the kitchen is a complete mess.)

Halve the zucchinis lengthwise, and if large cut the halves in half. Scoop out the pulp and save it.

Sauté chopped onions and garlic to a golden brown, and hold. Blend or chop (in blender or meat grinder) the spinach, parsley, and the scooped-out pulp of the zucchini. Add salt and pepper and sauté for a few minutes with the onion and garlic. Remove from heat and add the minced peppers and celery. Hold this while you beat some eggs for a stiffening of the whole mixture. Mix it all together, adding the beaten eggs.

The zucchini shells are very difficult to handle—they're limp and have too much water in them. Your aim is to have everything as dry as possible, because squash is a watery vegetable.

After you struggle putting this complete mixture in the zucchini halves, or half-halves, top with bread crumbs. Fill the zucchini generously with all of this, mound it up over the top, covering the edges of the squash, so the stuffing flavor will permeate the rind of the squash.

For freezing, place the stuffed zucchinis in the freezer overnight. When they're frozen, wrap each stuffed section in a plastic freezer bag and close the ends with a freezer tie. Later, if you put the frozen separate bags in a larger plastic bag you can easily pick out graceful and uniform sizes.

I'll answer this question now: There seems to be no smell of garlic in the freezing or the freezer. I think that the wrapping after the freezing takes care of it.

I find that vegetable oil rather than butter or margarine or olive oil holds longer in the freezer, and there's no fear it will get rancid. I notice that when I take the zucchini from the freezer I need to add more bread crumbs, butter, and more garlic. (Garlic seems to lose some of its flavor when frozen, although it still smells like garlic.) Grated cheese is marvelous on top, if you want to add that. These frozen zucchinis need not be defrosted. They can be put right in the oven at a moderate temperature, 325°–350°, until the squash rind is tender and a fork will pierce it, and the bread crumbs are golden brown.

For immediate eating, the zucchinis can be topped with buttered crumbs and either grated cheese or thin slices of cheddar cheese. Bake uncovered in a shallow pan at 350° until the squash shell is tender when pierced with a fork, and the cheese-and-crumb topping is brown.

I would think that for 6 medium zucchinis, which will make 12 halves, you will need 3 beaten eggs, 3 medium-size onions, 2 garlic cloves, 4 cups of cooked spinach, plus the pulp from the zucchinis. All the other ingredients, bread crumbs, cheese, celery, green peppers, and so on, can vary.

TOMATO-HERB CASSEROLE

This freezes so well that I always see to it that I have a few casseroles on hand, made when tomatoes are plentiful in the garden or inexpensive in the market. I've made it in the winter with canned tomatoes, but I'm always surprised at the amount of stewed tomatoes necessary, at a time when tomatoes are precious. (To make stewed tomatoes, peel the tomatoes, cut them in chunks in a little water, and heat them until you have tomatoes with juice.) You will need:

Stewed tomatoes
Cheddar cheese
White bread
Onion
Garlic tips or pressed garlic bulbs
Sugar
Butter
Salt and pepper
Any herbs you like—my choice of herbs is always oregano, thyme, and rosemary

Dice slices of white bread. Place a layer in a large flat casserole. Sprinkle the herbs on the bread (never a heavy hand with herbs). Add dots of butter, a little sugar, salt, pepper, garlic, and an unusually thinly sliced onion. Add some stewed tomatoes with their juice. Your aim is to repeat layers of bread, herbs and seasoning, and tomatoes, then top with thin slices of cheese.

For the freezer I do not precook this casserole. I want just as much of the fresh tomato taste as I can get, come winter. The cheese will brown nicely when the casserole is defrosted, then baked in a medium-hot oven. A 350° oven temperature for ¾ hour should be enough cooking time, unless you slice the onions too thick.

For immediate eating, bake and serve.

ENTRÉES (MAIN DISHES)

GLORY CHICKEN STEW

With young garden white onions and baby carrots and new potatoes, a summer heat wave upon us, I wanted to prepare a one-dish meal in the cool of the morning and then stay out of the hot kitchen. Stew was the logical answer; lamb or beef seemed too heavy in the heat; so I experimented with chicken. And ended up with one of the most delicious and exotic recipes I've ever made. It can be made any time of year and it should have another name, but I still call it Glory Chicken Stew. It is the most economical penny-pinching dish I know of. If you're interested in economy.

In theory it is one meal out of one chicken. In actuality that one chicken is so meltingly tender—skin, bones and all—and the sauce so rich, that one chicken stretches into three meals for two or one meal for six. If you want to stretch it still further, serve with noodles or rice or toast points. (Every time I make it, I am reminded of the box that was found in an old lady's attic labeled "pieces of string too short to use.") It can be warmed up over and over and still be good. It should freeze well, but I've never had a chance to try freezing it because we just kept eating it till it was gone.

You will need:

1 Fryer or broiler
1 Can cream-of-mushroom soup
2 Cups of milk
Small whole carrots
Small onions
New potatoes

Parsley or chives
Butter
Salt and pepper

Cut a broiler or fryer into small portions—wings, drumsticks, thighs, half or quarter the breast meat, the back cut in half, use the neck. But no giblets go in.

Broil the chicken pieces, buttered and salted and peppered, till they are rich golden brown on both sides. (It's really cooked, broiled chicken ready to eat at this point.)

Next, in an electric skillet or a frying pan, arrange the chicken pieces skin side up. (I never use the butter drippings from the pan, which would make the sauce overrich.) Add a can of cream-of-mushroom soup and two cups of milk. I just stir the milk and soup around the chicken pieces—the sauce will thicken by itself. Cover. Simmer. This can simmer for two or three hours or more. The only thing to allow for is that you have a deep enough skillet to take the vegetables later.

About an hour before meal time I add small whole carrots and small onions and scraped new potatoes. Keep simmering until the vegetables are tender and the flavors will have blended into a rich sauce. It doesn't much matter whether or not the vegetables are still whole. I add no extra seasoning because the bland taste of the sauce is what gives the recipe unusual delicacy and flavor. On serving, sprinkle some minced parsley or chopped chives over the top.

GARDEN BAKED CHICKEN

One winter day I found myself in a spot. I had invited a guest for dinner. I knew he was a hearty eater. It was 4 o'clock in the afternoon and he was due at 7. I racked my brains trying to figure out what to do. Then I thought of my freezer casseroles. I got out two casseroles from the freezer: one of Baked Garden Chicken, the other corn pudding. I took off their foil covers, covered them with Pyrex covers and put them in the oven at 200°. They were defrosted by six. Taking off the covers to let them brown, I raised the temperature to 350° and we ate at 7. The dinner was a success. So now I know I don't have to defrost my casseroles all day, which I had previously done. Voilà! Three hours from freezer to table.

For Garden Baked Chicken, you will need:

A cut-up, plump fowl
Small onions
Small whole baby carrots
One or two cans of button mushrooms
Flour
Milk
Salt, pepper, and paprika

Put the flour in a paper bag, adding salt and pepper and paprika. Put chicken pieces, a few at a time, in the paper bag. Hold the bag by the top and shake till the chicken is well coated with the flour-salt-pepper-paprika mixture. Sauté the chicken pieces in vegetable oil till they are golden brown. Remove and arrange in a casserole. Don't use the chicken drippings, because the foul will be rich enough with its own fat. Add milk to half cover the chicken pieces. Bake in a 350° oven and when the chicken is golden brown on one side, turn the pieces over and add the carrots, onions, and drained mushrooms. Bake until the chicken is tender when tested with a fork. Sprinkle the chopped parsley on top and serve in the casserole.

This dish can be allowed to overcook, but watch that the sauce doesn't bubble too much or it might curdle a bit. There's no effect on the taste if the milk curdles, but it doesn't look as pretty. Crunchy bread makes a good texture to go with this chicken. And with a salad you have a whole meal. A "real" dessert makes too heavy a meal, so I usually follow with a plate of fresh fruit and assorted cheeses, or Blender Ice-Tray Sherbet.

HURRICANE STEW

Come fall, if the radio warns of hurricane signals posted from Cape Hatteras to Cape Cod, I immediately react. I seem to feel the atmospheric pressure ahead of time, even though we're inland. I know that I begin to think in terms of candles and battening down the hatches and what food do we have for a couple of days' eating, and what is out in the garden. Inevitably, I make lamb stew—eating food, which can be warmed up over a can of Sterno or over the fireplace or the auxiliary gas stove in the basement if the electricity goes off. I get young baby carrots and young onions and parsley out of the garden. The commissary department must be prepared. My Hurricane Stew is always lamb stew. I don't know why.

You will need:

Lamb
Carrots
Onions
Celery
Rosemary

Parsley

Salt and pepper

Put cut-up lamb (with bones for flavor—the bones will be taken out later) in cold water with salt and pepper, and bring to a simmer. With a spoon remove the scum that comes to the top. When the lamb is tender, add whole young carrots, whole young onions, chunks of celery, and rosemary, and simmer till the vegetables are fork-tender. Serve with minced parsley sprinkled on top.

The celery is the secret of the flavor. It takes away any mutton taste which is always a hazard with lamb.

Stew is considered a luxury dish in our household. You can use any kind of stewing lamb, breast of lamb, or the combination deals, but we have happily cut up shoulder, rib, or loin chops for stew meat. Particularly when it's Hurricane Stew.

After the bones are removed, the stew juice can be thickened into a gravy. Make a paste of equal amounts of cold butter and flour and stir until smooth, adding a bit of the lamb stew juice at a time, and more parsley, then combining with the stew.

Dumplings can be added. Or potatoes. But I'm cooking ahead of a hurricane. And I want to go out and watch the wind.

GARDEN MEATLOAF

One day I was about to make a meatloaf. I had the hamburger and the other ingredients ready, when I thought of that lovely garden out there with its lush vegetables. So I decided to try a different kind of meatloaf, with the assistance of my garden. The recipe I con-cocted worked and was equally delicious hot or cold.

After collecting tomatoes, a green pepper, parsley, and onions, and bringing them into the kitchen, I wondered where to start. Luckily, I had bacon in the house (I always top a meatloaf with bacon), and fresh bread (the heels are good under the meatloaf to catch the bacon drippings). I always cook a meatloaf in a pie plate, so I got that out and put two heels of bread in it. Then I reached for a large mixing bowl. I used these ingredients:

1 Lb. ground beef

2 Slices of fresh bread, crumbled (I use white bread)

4 Slices, or 1-inch cubes of cheese, crumbled. (I prefer cheddar for this recipe.)

2 Slices of bacon

2 Fresh tomatoes, peeled and cut into chunks

1 Small green pepper, seeded and chopped

1 Small stalk of celery with its leaves, chopped fine

2 Tablespoons of parsley, chopped fine

1 Medium onion, also chopped fine

2 Raw eggs

A little salt and pepper

Set aside the bacon for the topping, and mix all the other ingredients together in the bowl. (Two forks can be used for this, because the mixture is very sticky.) I shape the mixture into a mounded loaf in the pie plate, with the heels of bread underneath and the bacon on top, and bake it for ¾ hour at 400°. Discard the heels of bread before serving.

Before it's baked, this mixture will seem very soft because of the raw eggs and the juice from the tomatoes. However, it will have a special soufflé taste when cooked, and will solidify when cold.

If you serve Garden Meatloaf cold or use it for sandwiches, condiments are seldom necessary because of the blended flavor of the meatloaf.

This Garden Meatloaf turned out to be my favorite of all meat-loaves.

LA SPINA

It all came about because the Baroness had an ulcerated tooth. When I was invited to visit her, the tooth had been pulled, but the Baroness was eating only a soft diet. One of the things we ate was the casserole I'm going to tell you about. By the time I returned home I had begun to like La Spina. And after I'd worked out my own variation, my family agreed. This casserole is full of vitamins and nutrition, and is one of the most economical casseroles I have ever made.

You will need:

1 Lb. freshly ground hamburger
4 Cups cooked rice
5 Garden tomatoes, peeled and cut in chunks
2 Large onions
Butter or margarine

Place cooked rice in a large buttered ovenproof bowl, peel tomatoes, cut them in big chunks, add the hamburger, slice the onions very, very thin. Add salt and pepper and two or three chunks of butter. Mix together gently with two forks. (Hands are quicker, but hamburger should never be crushed for fear of toughening it.) Bake in 350° oven for about 45 minutes.

By this time the aroma from the kitchen should make you hungry enough to eat about half of it. If you have any left over, it is just as good warmed up the next day, but you may need to add some more tomato chunks or tomato juice. Rice dries out after its first cooking.

HOT VEGETABLE PLATE

The dreary vegetable plate served in restaurants may be a "Dieter's Delight" but it has no relation to my fresh-from-the-garden Hot Vegetable Plate.

In the first place, I would not dream of using that dead-looking poached egg in the middle of the platter. I use a broiled tomato (Tomate Provençal) as my centerpiece.

Color appeal for dieters and nondieters is very important, so the vegetables that surround the tomato must be chosen carefully. Beets are out. But you will need:

   1 *Ripe tomato*
   Cooked white cauliflower
   Cooked green bush beans
   Cooked garden carrots
   Cooked wax beans
   Bread crumbs
   Garlic

For Tomate Provençal, do not peel the tomato. Scoop out the whole center pulp. Mix a few buttered bread crumbs with the pulp (a spoonful of bread crumbs will not hurt the dieter). Put the crumb mixture back in the tomato and stick in 3 garlic cloves. Broil until the top bread crumbs are golden brown. The garlic-flavored tomato will add delicious flavoring to the vegetables, which I arrange around the outside, like a wheel, with the tomato in the center.

ESCALLOPED GREEN-CABBAGE CASSEROLE

I discovered this one by chance, as is the case with so many inter-esting recipes. It all came about because I liked creamed cabbage and Hal didn't. So every time I sliced and quick-boiled a green cab-bage from the garden, I would mentally plan on escalloped cabbage the next day. But the flavor of quick-boiled cabbage is so delicate that we never had any left.

One day I cooked two cabbages and hid one bowl of it in the refrigerator. Lunchtime came, and I felt a little sneaky about the whole thing. After all, what wife doesn't cook primarily the things her husband prefers. A compromise had to be made. So I made a thickish cream sauce, added the cooked sliced cabbage, opened a can of corned beef, put thickish chunks of corned beef with the creamed cabbage in a casserole, added buttered bread crumbs for a topping, baked it in the oven till the breadcrumbs were brown. Hal said I could make it any time I chose, and he'd buy it.

This quick and easy luncheon casserole should be equally good with leftover ham chunks or crisp fried bacon. Or with the crinkly Savoy cabbage. Can be made winter or summer, but in winter make it when those first new green cabbages arrive in the market. Not the coleslaw white solid heads, but the juicy green tender cabbages.

SAUCES

GARDEN SPAGHETTI SAUCE

This is something I will never willingly be without. If my garden should lack the amount of tomatoes, peppers, or onions needed, I would buy them. I have found the year-round use of this sauce wonderful in so many and diversified ways that it is worth it to me in terms of money or time.

I know full well that cooking the sauce down is going to be an all-day do, and the preparation will take more time than I want to allow. The house will reek of it for hours, and every burner on the stove will be used, so it's quick and easy meals on spaghetti-sauce day. By the time I've simmered the sauce all day I never want to see a tomato or a pepper or an onion again, and won't want to think of it again until it's frozen. But after that day of making the sauce, it is one of the most inviting things I have on hand. I prefer a basic mild spaghetti sauce with that fresh garden taste, over a bed of spaghetti or any pasta, or rice, and especially for Spanish omelets.

You will need:

Red ripe tomatoes
Green peppers
Onions
Garlic
Dried or fresh oregano (fresh oregano is stronger, so be wary of it)
Vegetable oil

You can always add mushrooms, other herbs, or more garlic when you are ready to heat it up and use it.

My proportions for spaghetti sauce must be approximate—but it always seems to turn out well.

Peel the tomatoes after dipping in boiling water and cooling under the faucet to the point you can handle them. Have plenty of pans ready to keep all the produce separate. It doesn't matter if the tomatoes are on the stewed side because they have to cook down anyway. The tomatoes can be sliced or cut in chunks, waiting.

Peel and cut up onions in slices, take the seeds out of the peppers, then cut them in chunks. Sauté the onions in vegetable oil—not brown, but just transparent. Add the tomatoes and some of the chopped peppers. (Hold some of the peppers till the tomatoes and onions and oil have simmered down for two or three hours.) Use plenty of salt and pepper, put whole garlic bulbs in so that you can find them to take out later before freezing. Add a little oregano.

When the tomato and pepper and onion mixture has cooked down, combine in a big kettle, to simmer, until you have both the flavor and the consistency you want.

The approximate proportions for this would be five cups of chopped onions to five cups of chopped green peppers to six quarts of tomatoes.

The sauce may have to cook several hours longer. Then add more chopped green peppers for about half an hour, so you have the green-pepper look, which enhances both appearance and flavor.

There are no hazards to this recipe. Just time, a house reeking of spaghetti sauce, and every pan in the kitchen dirty. Fortunately, the acid of the tomatoes will have cleaned up the inside of every pan or container you've used. Which is a bonus.

I wouldn't think of making this for an immediate recipe. There's too much cooking. But it's wonderful to have in the freezer. I freeze it in Mason jars, pints or quarts, working carefully to leave headroom in the jars to avoid any possible cracking. Individual servings can be frozen in freezer bags or small plastic containers.

CHILI SAUCE

I'm not a pickler by nature. But one recipe is so wonderful for Spanish omelets, hot dogs, or hamburgers, that although it takes a long time to prepare the garden vegetables and simmer and watch the sauce, I like to have it on hand. I double it, triple it, or quadruple the recipe, and if my green peppers have not yet turned red, it is worth the expenditure of buying them. Both for color and flavor.

You will need:

12 Red ripe tomatoes
4 Onions
4 Sweet red peppers
2 Cups cider vinegar
1 Tablespoon salt
½ Cup sugar
1 Tablespoon celery seed
1 Teaspoon each of cinnamon, cloves, allspice, and nutmeg

Peel the tomatoes and slice. Chop peppers and onion. Cook until reduced by half. Just before removing from the heat, add the vinegar, sugar, and spices. Let boil up once and seal in sterile Mason jars.

 DESSERTS

BLENDER ICE-TRAY SHERBET

This is so easy to make that I always try to have a tray of it in the refrigerator. The smooth tangy flavor is particularly good with a heavy main meal and is especially refreshing as a dessert on a summer day.

You will need:

> *Whites of two or three eggs*
> *½–¾ Cup of finely chopped ice*
> *1 Large can of frozen lemonade concentrate*
> *1–2 Tablespoons fresh lime juice*

Put all the ingredients in the blender and beat long enough to be very creamy, at least 2 minutes at high speed. Pour in an ice tray and freeze.

For the finely chopped ice we use the slivers of ice in the bottom of our ice-cube container. Any method of crushing ice or chopping it fine can be used. The only thing to watch out for is to beat the mixture long enough. It should have a frothy mousselike consistency so that the ice particles will not settle to the bottom of the ice tray when frozen.

I have tried this recipe with frozen orange juice, frozen berries or fruit of all kinds, but I always come back to the lemon and lime combination. I was lucky enough to find ice-cube trays with individual plastic ice-cube molds which made serving the sherbet much simpler and more festive-looking.

OTHER DESSERT IDEAS

For complicated desserts, you are on your own. I find that assorted cheeses and slices of apple (I have apple trees) are always welcome after a hearty meal. The best way to serve apples is to slice them through, then put the slices back together in apple form. The result will look inviting, and the individual slices will be easy to spread with cheese. I usually serve several cheeses, because people have favorites—from rat cheese (Cheddar) to Camembert to blue to Roquefort to Brie.

I also have a pear tree which furnishes fresh pears or pears in juice from the freezer. I freeze assorted melon balls in juice, whether I grow watermelons or cantaloupes or buy them.

There's always ice cream too. And if you are fortunate enough you may have strawberries for parfaits.

Index

Underlined page numbers refer to recipes.